PEN

FIT FO

It's the first week of a new term, a new life, in the sixth form at St Andrews Road School, commonly known as S.T.A.R.S. Well, you are a star, aren't you, once you're in the sixth form. Ella, Sam, Kirsty, Raffy, Colette, Dim and Jules have been together all the way through their comprehensive. But will life and loves change in the sixth? Who is that new and stunning girl, calling herself Taz? And Toby, ever so polite, what's he doing here?

As the first month progresses, it is Kirsty who feels she doesn't quite fit in, though she is getting physically fit at their all-women Saturday morning weight-training classes. Will she see the light? And what will she do with her powerful secret?

This is the first book in the S.T.A.R.S. sequence. Every month there will be a new, self-contained story, all about the same group of sixth formers. S.T.A.R.S. is about real life inside a modern London comprehensive. It's funny, action-packed and full of great characters. Join now. The common room door is always open. Waiting for you . . .

Hunter Davies is an author, journalist and broadcaster. He has written over thirty books, ranging from biographies of the Beatles to William Wordsworth, and he wrote the 'Father's Day' column in *Punch* for ten years. He is the author of the *Flossie Teacake* stories and has also written a book for teenagers, *Saturday Night*. He has three children and lives in London.

Canal
St Andrews Road Church
old building
New building
Library
Head's Study
St Andrew's Place
ST. ANDREWS SCHOOL
Shah's Newsagents
Caretaker's House
Redgras Sports surface
Tennis Courts
Sixth-form Common-room
St Andrews Road
Fred's Cafe
Camden Town
Hampstead Heath
Bus stop No 24
The Cow and Bull Pub

Fit for the Sixth

HUNTER DAVIES

PENGUIN BOOKS

PENGUIN BOOKS

Published by the Penguin Group
27 Wrights Lane, London W8 5TZ, England
Viking Penguin Inc., 40 West 23rd Street, New York, New York 10010, USA
Penguin Books Australia Ltd, Ringwood, Victoria, Australia
Penguin Books Canada Ltd, 2801 John Street, Markham, Ontario, Canada L3R 1B4
Penguin Books (NZ) Ltd, 182–190 Wairau Road, Auckland 10, New Zealand

Penguin Books Ltd, Registered Offices: Harmondsworth, Middlesex, England

First published in 1989
10 9 8 7 6 5 4 3

Filmset in Linotron Ehrhardt by
Rowland Phototypesetting Ltd,
Bury St Edmunds, Suffolk
Printed and bound in Great Britain by
Cox and Wyman Ltd, Reading, Berks.

Sam: feeling strange

EPISODE 1

Outside St Andrews School, very early September. It's the first day for all new sixth formers, the first day of their new school year, the first day of their new life . . .

Raffy and Sam are standing at the front gates, feeling self-conscious and a bit strange, but not knowing why. After all, for five whole years they have come through these self-same gates.

'This is really weird, man,' says Raffy. 'Where's everyone?'

'How about taking your shades off?' says Sam. 'That might help.'

Raffy takes them off for a second, then puts them on again, realizing at last why it all seems so strange. There are no hordes of younger kids swirling around, in particular no younger girls he can chat up, make personal remarks about, shout lewd comments at. Today is the first day of school, but for sixth formers only. They are about to be Inducted. Tomorrow, the real rabble will arrive.

Raffy is dark-haired and slim, cocky and confident, but he needs an audience of some sort to give himself an identity. He does have a good seven o'clock shadow, verging on the ten past eight which was when he got up, so that helps the image, and a bandana round his head, but he fears that might have become old-fashioned the moment he put it on.

Sam has short, mousy hair and a mousy sort of smile, which he's working on, as he knows he normally looks shy and hesitant. He's wearing a brand-new polo shirt, bought by his mum for his first day back, as if he were a first-year kid. He's waiting for the smart-ass comments from people like Raffy, who'll no doubt say it looks yuppie, or even worse, private school.

Sam is a bit more hesitant than usual today. Not because of his clothes. He's wondering what the sixth form will be like: will he cope, will he fail, will he be found out. Sam knows he has done nothing to be ashamed of – well hardly. It's just that he has always felt on the verge of being found out, not for anything in particular, just for living and breathing.

'There's something funny about you,' says Raffy.

'Thanks,' says Sam. 'Wish I could say the same about you.'

'No, I mean, stand over there, let's look at you.'

'Get lost,' says Sam.

All the same, he steps back a few paces. Will it be his shirt, or his flies undone, or dog shit on his new trainers, or even worse, has he come out with the wrong hair cut? Perhaps he shouldn't have had it as short and brutal. At least he didn't have any of his hair shaved.

'It's your stupid Spurs bag,' says Raffy.

Sam is relieved that all Raffy can find to comment on is his sports bag, the battered and tattered old holdall he has carted his stuff to school in for the last four years. In the first year there was a spell, which he dare hardly think about now, when he had a briefcase – real leather, bought by his grandmother – which he took proudly with him for his first term, till he learned better. Looking back, it was probably Raffy who first pointed out his gross error, then piled on the ridicule. All the same, his mother made him take it for the rest of the year. He has still not forgiven her.

'Right,' says Sam. 'I'll have a quid on with you now that Spurs will end up higher in the League than Arsenal.'

'I'm not talking about Spurs, dum dum,' says Raffy, 'but about your Spurs *bag*, any bag in fact.'

'What you on about?' says Sam, not really interested, beginning to wonder if the real reason no one is around is that everyone else has already gone inside, leaving him and Raffy to enter the New World on their own.

'Where have you been all your life?' says Raffy. 'Oh I forgot, you were in the Lake District, trying to sleep with your favourite sheep. No wonder you're out of touch. Just as long as you had a good wash afterwards.'

'I think we should go in,' says Sam.

'Not like that,' says Raffy. 'You're an embarrassment. I'll have to pretend I'm not with you.'

Raffy delves into the back pocket of his jeans, making a big performance of it, bending and arching his body as his jeans are so tight. He manages to slip his hand down at last and pulls out a small comb which falls on the ground.

'Forgot about that,' says Raffy, picking it up. 'No use to you of course, squire. But then you don't need to look pretty, not for sheep.'

Sam swings his Spurs bag at him, just as they used to do, oh, many years ago, when Raffy came to school with his Arsenal sports bag, back in the dark ages of the fifth year.

Raffy leans over again, managing more contortions and further moans and groans, till he brings forth a plastic bag, just a simple, ordinary, workaday plastic bag, the sort you get free at supermarkets. He shakes it high in the air, letting the air unfold it. Sam and the world at large can now see that Raffy, or someone connected with him, has recently been a customer of J. Sainsbury.

'Oh God, I forgot,' says Sam. 'I did mean to, but with being away, I never sort of got it together this morning . . .'

'Well if we're going in now, just don't walk with me, that's all,' says Raffy.

Sam should have remembered of course. The mystique and the magic, the rituals and rites, the privileges and the powers of life and love in the sixth form take many forms, most of them still waiting to be unfolded. But there is one trivial custom favoured by most sixth-form boys, which Raffy and Sam observed while still fresh-faced fifth formers. This concerns plastic bags. Just ordinary supermarket plastic bags. Last year, and things could well have changed now, they were what the well-dressed sixth former used for carrying around his worldly goods and possessions.

'You haven't got a spare one?' asks Sam, wondering if he should dump his Spurs bag at once. Since the end of the golden age of Hoddle, he hasn't been so keen to drag it around anyway.

'Nope, it's my only one,' says Raffy. 'I didn't think ahead.'

'God, I'll look a right jerk when we get in the common room,' says Sam.

'Okay then,' says Raffy. 'As you are my best and oldest and probably most backward mate, I'll do you a big favour. As it is our first day.'

Raffy takes the Spurs bag from Sam's hand, bends it in half, which is quite easy as there is so little inside, and stuffs it into his Sainsbury's plastic carrier.

'Right,' says Raffy. 'Are you happy, sunshine?'

And so Raffy and Sam walk slowly into school.

Then more confidently. Then at a quick trot, breaking into a gallop as they realize that the absence of other people around does mean they are already late for the first day of their new life.

Moments later, inside the sixth-form common room

One group is listening to loud reggae music on a stereo, others are playing cards, chess, backgammon, reading newspapers or paperbacks. Some are lying on the floor, others on cushions, but most are standing up, jostling and moving around, looking out old friends.

'It's like being at university,' says Ella.

'How do you know?' says Kirsty. 'You've never been.'

'A foreign university,' says Colette. 'A sort of students' union in one of those funny European countries.'

'Well at least I look the part,' says Kirsty. 'Dunno about you two.'

Kirsty has decided to dress like an art student, or how she thinks an art student should dress, with very white make-up, a very short miniskirt and dark tights with holes in them. The effect, thinks Ella, is tarty, rather than arty, but she is too polite to say so.

Colette has gone more for modern fashion, she thinks, basing her ensemble on a feature in *Just Seventeen*, though without quite the same purchasing power. Her top is a special offer, floppy, black and yellow T-shirt, only £4.99. She could not afford the recommended yellow leggings to go with it, so she's created her own out of a pair of jumble pyjamas, which are already beginning to split.

Ella is dressed well, sweetly, like most parents would want their lower-sixth daughter to look: clean and neat, nothing extreme, nothing aggressive, but not cheap. Benetton skirts and tops are not given away.

Almost all the boys appear to be in the same uniform: jeans, trainers, T-shirt or shirt, but oh the agonies behind some of those apparently simple decisions.

'Where's Sam?' says Colette to Ella.

'I dunno,' says Ella. 'I'm not his keeper.'

'But you'd like to be,' says Colette.

'Shurrup,' says Ella. 'He's always late anyway. That's why I didn't call for him.'

'Ooh, what's that funny smell?' asks Kirsty.

'Could be your make-up,' says Colette. 'You're not supposed to use pan stick from an actual frying pan.'

Kirsty sniffs the air, then she turns and looks out into the garden. Three boys are leaning against the door smoking a cigarette, home-rolled by the look of it, taking turns to have a puff.

'I didn't know you could smoke in the sixth form,' says Kirsty.

'You can,' says Colette. 'But not actually in the common room. You have to go outside in the yard, they don't mind that. It's one of the privileges.'

'I heard what you said there,' mumbles one

of the smoking boys, coming through the door.

'Me? I didn't speak,' says Kirsty, aggressively. 'Not to you, anyway.' She is half-expecting some facetious remark about her outfit, and is ready to get in first with an appropriately rude mouthful; just to establish herself as a person who might look as if liberties can be taken, but isn't one to be put down easily.

'There are no privileges in the sixth form,' says the boy, stopping and looking at Colette. 'We call them facilities.'

'Sor-ree,' says Colette.

'And there are no powers either,' says the boy. 'We don't do any duties, or give any punishments. Privileges and power imply we're something special, which is what too many people in this world think they are. We're not special, nobody is. These pathetic facilities are what everyone in this lousy school should have . . .'

He turns round, makes a sweeping gesture round the room, then falls over.

'Thanks for the lecture,' says Colette, keeping her face straight. She and Kirsty then burst out laughing, clutching each other. Ella nudges them, trying to shut them up in case the boy hears them and is upset. He slowly gets to his feet and shuffles off without turning round again.

In another corner of the sixth-form common room

Dim is pushing his way around, in and out of the

groups. This is quite easy for him, being big and burly, but he tries not to push too much. There seem to be quite a few people he doesn't know, new to the school, plus some who have been hiding in corners all these years and now suddenly seem to have grown up, acquired a persona and a style.

'Ugh,' grunts Dim, as he goes round. This is his nearest equivalent to an apology. 'Huh,' grimaces Dim. This is the nearest he gets to a big hello, blurting it out on seeing someone he does happen to know well.

Jules is also making his way around, but ever so suavely, ever so politely, with a word for everyone, whether he knows them or not. He is busy observing any new clothes, commenting on a new hairstyle or a good tan, congratulating some people on good exam results, or commiserating with others.

'I've just heard, darling,' he is saying to one girl. 'What pigs they are. And like pigs, I must fly.'

'I do like your shoes,' he says to a boy with bare feet. 'Wish I could do that, but I haven't got the ankles.'

'Yes, this afternoon, in the caff-ay,' he answers someone else, pronouncing the word correctly, giving it the full French acute accent. Everyone else calls it 'the caff', which is what it is, a greasy transport café just along from the school, traditionally the haunt of the sixth form.

'So I'll see you then,' goes Jules. 'Laters.' This is his new smart phrase, 'laters'. He likes to have a different one every term, moving on the moment the rest of the school catches up.

'My God, Dmitri,' screams Jules. 'What have you done with your hair?'

Dim feels it to check it's there, just in case anything might have happened to it since the last time he saw it, which was some time ago.

'Whachamean?' grunts Dim, almost, but not quite, giving Jules a welcome smile. They too have been through the whole of primary and secondary school together.

'Done nuffink wif it,' says Dim. His affectation is to speak worse than he would naturally, deciding that as a scientist, he has no need to use the English language properly.

'That's precisely the point,' says Jules. 'But you should, you should.'

'Why?' says Dim.

'This is the sixth form,' says Jules, 'don't you know.'

Back on the couch, with the girls

'Who's that poser in the suit?' says Colette, still on the couch. 'I can only see his back.'

'I think he looks quite tasty,' says Kirsty.

'My God, look who it is,' says Ella.

They all jump up, screaming, and rush towards the smartly suited figure of Jules. Dim has not even commented on his new outfit.

'I thought no one would ever notice,' says Jules. He twirls round to give them all the benefit of the cut.

'You look brilliant,' says Colette.

In turn, the girls all give Jules a kiss. Colette also manages to give a little kiss to Dim, as they are supposed to be going out. She knows that Dim is not keen on too much show of emotion, at least not in the football season, when he should be in training.

There is then more yelling and screaming when they spot Sam and Raffy, and more kissing ensues. In the sixth form, it is generally done to be ecstatic when meeting one's friends after an absence, even after a weekend. Sometimes just after a free period.

Raffy picks Kirsty up by the waist and swings her round, which she enjoys, despite protesting loudly.

'Knickers on, I see,' he says. 'Well I suppose it is the first day of term.'

'Cheeky sod,' says Kirsty, giving him a pretend slap.

'I thought at first you were the school doctor,' says Raffy, turning to Jules in his suit. 'Come to check us all for AIDS.'

'Well I have to try so hard,' says Jules, 'to match you three guys for sartorial elegance.'

Sam is in jeans, like Dim and Raffy, but he has made an extra effort and put on his new shirt, the one bought by his mum. Ella gives him an extra kiss. 'Love your shirt,' she says.

'Shurrup,' says Sam sharply. He is pleased she has noticed it, but does not want it to attract further attention.

'Oh, be like that,' says Ella, drawing away.

'Didn't mean it like that,' says Sam, trying to pull her towards him, but she gets free.

'Now, now, children,' says Jules. 'This is a happy day. And just to prove I am in the sixth form, as well as you infants, I have brought my badge with me.' He opens his jacket and from the inside pocket pulls a neatly rolled-up green plastic bag.

'Oh yeah,' says Dim. 'I got a green one as well.' He unrolls a green plastic carrier from his pocket, one of St Michael's medium-sized ones.

'Marks and Spencer,' says Raffy. 'How boring.'

Jules's bag is best-quality green plastic, thick and heavy, beautifully printed as befits an item from Sotheby's. They all jeer and laugh, which Jules enjoys, and they enjoy too. Jules, unlike some of them, can take a joke at his own expense.

Seven old friends, happy to see each other again, happy to look forward to an eventful term.

Taz: what a vision

EPISODE 2

Later, in the school hall

Lionel Witting, Head of the Sixth, is giving his annual pep talk. He explains the rules and regulations, conduct and conditions, how everyone must follow some course, either for A levels, re-sits, or a CPVE vocational course. It is an open sixth form, with no one refused entry because of poor exam results. 'But those who do no work will not be allowed to stay. Is that clear? Is that understood?' Mr Witting has given the same talk every year for the last ten years, but he still manages to throw himself into it with enthusiasm.

'Boring, boring,' mutters Raffy.

'Shut up,' says Sam. 'I'm listening.'

They have managed, all seven of them, to sit in

the same row. Raffy is concentrating on making smart remarks. Jules concentrates on his suit, worrying if sitting down for so long will play hell with his creases. Dim is picking the team for his first match as football captain, and having some difficulty with the subs. Can he possibly include Sam, his old friend, or is he really too weak and weedy, however keen?

'Get on with it,' says Raffy.

Mr Witting pauses at the end of a lengthy description of the six Certificate of Pre-Vocational Education courses on offer. Then he goes into an explanation of the sixth-form common room, how the facilities must not be absued, how they are on trust. Ella and Colette note his use of the word 'facilities', not 'privileges'.

'Oh God,' groans Raffy. 'We know all this . . .'

It is almost as if Mr Witting has heard Raffy, because he then apologizes for going over points which old S.T.A.R.S. (long pause, foxy smile), i.e. people used to St Andrews Road School, will already know well.

'But there are amongst us today,' he continues, 'quite a few people who are completely new to the school. I offer them a warm welcome and hope they will be happy here. As happy as we all are . . .'

He finishes on a smile, and everyone gives a mock sarcastic groan at his last remark. Then the Head, Mrs Potter, takes over to explain some new GCSE re-sit regulations.

'Hey, where are all these new people?' says Raffy.

He turns round, squeaking his chair deliberately and holding out his arms, about to groan and hide his eyes in pretend horror at all the scruffy rabble behind him.

He finds himself staring into the face of a beautiful girl, her long legs gracefully curled just a few feet from his back, dressed in a pair of designer jeans.

She is not looking at him, despite their close proximity. Her gaze is fixed miles away. From time to time she makes a few notes on an ornate pad, using a real pen with real ink. She appears not to have noticed Raffy and from her expression, it looks as if she never will.

'Oh my God,' cries Raffy. 'It's a vision!'

He is turning so far round in his chair, straining to get a proper view, that the chair collapses. This is partly the work of Dim, fed up with Raffy's endless interruptions. He has given Raffy's chair a kick, with his stronger, goal-scoring right foot.

Mrs Potter stops her talk and waits for the noise to cease, noting that Raphael is the cause of it, just as he so often was in the fifth year. She decides to ignore him, denying him the satisfaction of any further attention.

'Help, I'm injured,' groans Raffy. 'Someone, lift me up.' He is hoping of course that the Apparition of Beauty will condescend to assist him, or at least acknowledge his existence, but she is busy making another elegant note on her elegant pad. Raffy struggles to his feet, putting his chair straight and causing further disturbance before he settles down again.

'Dim,' he mutters loudly, 'she's fantastic. Get a butcher's.'

Only Raffy has turned round so far. Sam, Dim and Jules assume it's one of Raffy's silly jokes, and that there will be no one there, or someone incredibly unattractive.

'Sam, wait till you see her,' says Raffy. 'Wow!'

The girls slyly turn their heads as Mrs Potter continues with her speech. They give the merest glance, as if checking the time, looking for a friend, searching the floor for something, not of course looking at *Her*.

'Huh,' says Kirsty, unable to resist a comment if only to counter Raffy. 'She's too thin.'

'You can never be too thin,' says Jules. He turns round now, realizing somebody worth seeing must be there. He does this openly, staring into the girl's face and giving her one of his friendliest, nicest smiles. She smiles back, politely, graciously, but not exactly warmly, like a princess on official duty, then returns to her notepad.

'You can never be too thin,' says Jules again. 'Or too rich.'

'Gawd,' says Raffy, gawping once again, his mouth open. 'I think she is rich as well. Oh my Gawd. She's got everything . . .!' He closes his eyes, pretending to faint, slowly slumping forward on his chair. At last, he is silent.

Later, in the tutor group

The seven friends are quite pleased. They have managed to stay together in the same tutor group, with Ken Grott as their tutor. He has a strong South London accent, a skinhead haircut, an earring, and always wears a CND badge on his very worn pullover. He teaches Sociology and plays the saxophone, often at the same time, if he thinks the Head, or the dreaded Mr Banks, one of the Deputy Heads, are a long way away. Not that a tutor really matters in the sixth form. The tutor group is merely a focal point, a place to hang your hat, check in your name.

The boys are especially pleased, well chuffed, because the mysterious Asian girl is in their group. She turns out to be called Taz, though no one is quite sure how the name is spelled or what it stands for.

The girls are not quite so over the moon. They have still to decide on what they think about Taz. She has not spoken to any of them yet. There is also a body of opinion which suspects that Mr Grott, who has never taught them before, could be two-faced, despite his image as 'Friend to all Sixth Formers, Call me Ken'.

'Kirsty,' says Mr Grott, wandering round and flicking through sheets of paper, looking for something. 'Oh Gawd, what crap I get lumbered with every year. Why do I bother? Oh, here it is. Bad news, Kirsty. You're on the probation list.'

'You what?' says Kirsty.

Mr Grott goes over to her and explains slowly and kindly that it's just a formality, and she must not be upset. Around a dozen of the new Sixth every year, out of over a hundred, are put on what's called probation, just till half-term.

'It's one of Mr Banks's systems, to scare everyone into submission,' he says. 'It's just for those who might not, just might not, be on the right course.'

'So, who says I'm not?' says Kirsty, aggressive and rather angry.

'Not me, keep your wig on,' says Mr Grott, going through more papers. 'It's probably these GCSE grades. You're being allowed to start A-level Art and also, hold on, what's the other one, oh yeah, Sociology, thanks to me, despite some not exactly brilliant results. The school rule is that you must have at least four grade Cs to do A levels. They don't want you to be overtaxed, to take on too much, that's all it is.'

'Well they can stuff it,' says Kirsty.

'Don't be like that,' replies Mr Grott. 'Anyway, see how it goes, and if you have any problems, see Mr Witting. He'll sort things out. That's his pigeon. I don't know anything. I just work here.'

He opens a drawer, and shoves all the papers untidily inside. 'Right,' he looks round. 'I suppose I'd better say it once again, for those who were asleep in the hall, or playing silly buggers with their chairs. Lionel Witting, as Head of the Sixth, is the person to answer any problems about your UCCA or PCAS forms, if and when you get round to them.

You know what they're for: admission to university, poly, tech. college, or Borstal, if that's where you fancy going.'

'And what's your pigeon, Ken?' says Raffy, already in the swing of being a sixth former, determined to treat the staff like ordinary humans – just as some of them appear, so far, to want to treat the students.

'I'm here to help with any other problems, personal, human problems, at least any of the sort which can be solved. Luckily, most personal problems can't, so I don't have much to do. There's only one answer for those sort of questions.'

'What's that, sir?' says Colette in a little girl voice, deliberately saying 'sir', so managing to keep her distance, mocking him, knowing he is just waiting to be asked.

'Life,' replies Mr Grott, sighing. 'The Big L. What they are pleased to call "the world out there". You can usually rely on living to cope with most problems, or at least to cover over the cracks.'

'Ooh, that's awfully profound,' says Raffy. 'I'll have to think about that. But if this thing called Life, you know, Biggish L, Biggish Hell, is so good, why have *you* missed out on it, huh?'

There is a smile of anticipation all round. There could be some good jostling bouts in the months ahead.

'All will be revealed,' says Mr Grott. 'Dinna worry yourself, my little Raphael.'

'Oh I'm not worried,' goes Raffy. 'Just call me

curious. Curious, Brown eyes, Camden Town. That's how I usually sign my personal agony letters to *Just Seventeen*. I've got a good one in this week, asking what to do when your condom splits. Perhaps you've seen it? I just signed it "Anon".'

'Not yet, I'm saving it for break,' says Mr Grott, briskly. 'Right. Any other questions? There are two newcomers here, so feel free to ask anything . . .'

Everyone turns round, having assumed till then that only Taz is new. She has been the centre of all their attention so far and the one for whom Raffy has really been performing, not Mr Grott, as he assumes. But at the back of the room sits a very young-looking boy, small, slight, fresh-faced, hardly more than thirteen, or so he appears. His hair is quite long, in an old-fashioned, neat style, his face rather large for his body, and he's wearing obviously new jeans and a very clean T-shirt.

'Just one little question, sir,' he says quietly, using the title naturally, not as a joke. 'If I may.'

'Yes, Toby,' says Mr Grott. 'Go right ahead.'

'Could you tell me, briefly, when is the next election to the School Council?'

They all give a loud groan, exaggerated, but meant. The School Council, in the opinion of most of them, is a joke. They have rubbished its very existence for the last five years.

Mr Grott opens his drawer, finds some more papers, and looks up the date. Toby thanks him politely.

'What a plonker,' says Raffy, rolling his eyes as if

dealing with an idiot and turning his back on the new boy. 'Which hole has he crept out of?'

Later, back in the common room

The room is now half-empty. School has finished early as today has been for the sixth form only, plus the new first years who are out there somewhere in another part of the St Andrews planet, being indoctrinated into the confusing first-year world. Most sixth formers are now filling their plastic bags, collecting any belongings and going home.

'Isn't he lovely?' says Colette.

'Lush,' says Kirsty.

'I do like his voice,' adds Ella.

'Talking about me again?' says Raffy. He is standing watching the door, reading *2000 AD*, but keeping an eye open for anyone coming in or out.

'And such nice manners,' says Ella. All three girls are lolling on the bashed-up couch, which they have decided to claim as their own.

'Terribly well spoken,' says Colette. 'My mum could go for him.'

'I thought she was fixed up,' says Kirsty.

'I mean for me,' says Colette. 'She would definitely approve of him for me, compared with some of the dum dums I get stuck with. Or should I say Dim Dims.'

Dim is not listening. He's sucking his pencil, about to pin a notice on the board.

'What's happened to your mum's bloke, anyway?' asks Kirsty. 'Are they still going out?'

'Not no more.'

'Two negatives make an affirmative,' says Jules.

'He chucked her,' Colette goes on, ignoring Jules as well. 'After they'd gone to Brighton.'

'Men are all the same,' says Kirsty. 'Pigs.'

'Ahh,' says Raffy. 'So yous are not talking about me after all.'

'Don't like his name, though,' says Ella. 'Toby – it's a bit sort of posh.'

'You mean it's not nice and chunky,' says Sam. 'Like Sam, for example.'

They are also ignoring Sam, though he has done nothing to annoy them so far.

'Have you found out his second name?' says Ella.

'It's his phone number we want,' says Colette.

'So we can ring him up and take down his particulars,' adds Kirsty. They all scream and laugh at this. Kirsty gives a particularly dirty snigger.

'Oh Gawd,' says Raffy. 'It's like listening to a load of old fishwives. I expect that of you, Kirsty, being a probationary, but I hoped for a higher level of conversation from the rest of you sixth formers, even if you are girls . . .'

Kirsty picks up a book and throws it at him. 'Piss off, bum face,' she says. 'Go and find your Taj Mahal Beauty. See what she thinks of you. If she even notices you exist.'

She throws another book at him, then one of the cushions. Raffy manages to dodge the missiles, then retreats through the common-room door. Colette and Ella stand up and collect their things, linking arms with Kirsty.

'Ah, such good friends,' says Jules.

The girls leave the common room together, comforting Kirsty, without saying cheerio, or even 'Laters', to any of the boys.

Kirsty: lend us a quid

EPISODE 3

One week later, Saturday morning, Kirsty's home

Kirsty lives with her parents, two older brothers and one younger sister, in a high-rise block. Her mother is cooking in the kitchen, where she spends most of her time.

'Mum, can you lend me £1.50?' asks Kirsty. She is finishing off her breakfast – toast and cereal, as opposed to nothing at all on school mornings. It's Saturday morning, a time when she needs all her strength.

'What for, dear?' says her mother.

'To spend.'

'I know that,' says her mother. 'I didn't think you were going to eat it.' She comes through carrying a large plate of fried eggs and bacon.

'Ugh, horrible,' says Kirsty. 'Take it out of my sight.'

'Where is he?' says her mother, looking around. 'I thought I heard him up.'

'Gone,' answers Kirsty. 'Emigrated, I hope.'

'Oh well,' says her mother, trudging back into the kitchen. 'I'd better put it in the micro and keep it hot for him. He does hate lukewarm bacon . . .'

'Mum!' shrieks Kirsty. 'You are a fool! Why do you run after them? Let them rot in their stinking beds.'

'I run after you as well, dear, don't forget.'

Kirsty returns to her toast, and her father's *Daily Express*. 'And I dunno why you get this crappy newspaper.'

'All you've done since you started that sixth form is criticize and moan,' says her mother.

'Well you deserve it,' says Kirsty savagely, then controls herself, remembering she still has to borrow £1.50.

'Look, why can't you sit down,' she goes on. 'Let them all fend for themselves. Or just make one meal, and say that's it, instead of waiting around all day for those pigs to appear.'

'And here I am,' says Kevin, her oldest brother, coming into the room still in his pyjama trousers, unshaven and scratching his lager belly. He gives pig-like grunting noises, just to annoy his sister even more.

'Oh God,' moans Kirsty.

'Chop chop, woman,' he says. 'I'm bloody starving.'

Their mother bustles around, gets Kevin's breakfast and places it on the dining table in front of him, where a place is already set. Their table is never unlaid, as there is always someone her mother is waiting to feed, just as there is always tea in the pot, and the kettle on, ever ready.

'You're a throwback, you know,' says Kirsty to her mother. 'Laws were passed to protect people like you. Women chained themselves to barriers, just to help you. What a waste of time that was.'

'I'm glad you're learning interesting things in the sixth form, dear,' says her mother, sweetly. 'Sorry, Kev, I forgot the sauce.'

'Where's your purse, Mum?' says Kirsty, getting up, ostentatiously clearing away her dishes and putting them neatly in their brand-new dishwasher, just to show Kevin.

'I don't know,' says her mother. 'I've been looking for it already.'

'You never know where anything is,' says Kirsty.

'That's true. Life goes past in a flash, and leaves me behind.'

'Oh no, don't give us the philosophy now,' says Kirsty. 'Just give us the money.'

'What did you say you needed it for?' asks her mother.

'I told you,' says Kirsty. 'My class.'

'What class? I thought the sixth form was free.'

'Oh Gawd,' moans Kirsty. 'I think you're going senile, you really are.'

'That's not very funny, Kirsten,' says her mother. 'Never make jokes about the afflicted.'

Kirsty's grandmother suffers from senile dementia, and lives nearby in a sheltered flat. Kirsty's mother goes every day to cook a meal for her, and Kirsty is also supposed to go and help, when she can.

'Huh,' she grunts, giving a sort of apology. 'Kev, can you lend me some money till Monday?'

'What for?' he asks.

'Oh God, not another bloody inquisition.'

'And don't swear,' says her mother.

Kirsty does not want to tell Kevin where she is going. He will merely mock, or use the information against her in some future row.

'Okay, forget it,' she says. 'Sorry I asked.'

Kevin stands up and lunges towards a pair of trousers, his best pair. They are on a wire coat hanger behind the door where he left them last night, ready for his mother to iron before he goes out again tonight.

'How much d'you want?' he says, pulling his trousers across the table, knocking over a milk bottle which his mother rushes to pick up.

'How much you got?' asks Kirsty.

'Loadsamoney,' says Kevin.

'I might have guessed that,' says Kirsty. 'Er, just a couple of quid will do.'

Kevin pulls out a wad of tenners and shoves one

towards her, going back to the sports pages of the newspaper.

'It's a present,' he says. 'From a pig.'

Meanwhile, Saturday morning over in Ella's home

Ella lives in a neat little terraced house. She is sitting in the kitchen drinking an orange juice, sugar-free, reading her weekend stars in last night's evening paper and wondering whether to wash her hair or not, a thought that is rarely far from her mind. The stars are no help, as washing hair is not mentioned.

Her father is setting out a breakfast tray, cutting toast into soldiers, very painstakingly, and carefully watching an egg boiling and burbling in a pan of water. He has done this every Saturday morning of Ella's life, as far as she can remember. It is the little treat he gets for his wife before going out to work. Ella's father is a taxi driver.

'And where you going, madam?' he asks.

'Out,' says Ella.

'With Sam?' says her father.

'Could be,' says Ella.

'I haven't seen him round recently.'

'That's because I keep him away if you're around,' says Ella.

'Thanks,' says her father.

'Well, you would just hassle him, asking him stupid questions.'

'No I wouldn't!'

'You always have done,' says Ella. 'That's why I sneak him into my bedroom in the middle of the night when you're asleep.'

Her father pauses, unsure for a moment if this is a joke or not. 'Wouldn't surprise me,' he says. 'I dunno what's happened to you since you started that sixth form.'

'Not that again.'

Sam is Ella's first boyfriend, real boyfriend. They have been through school together, but just as friends. They only got together recently. Ella has the details in her diary. In code, of course, one which she hopes her father will never crack.

'What's that Spurs bag for?' says her father.

'Nothing,' says Ella.

'Can't be for nothing. Have you got your saxophone in it?'

'Don't be stupid,' says Ella. 'It's just my things.'

'What things?'

'Oh you know, when you go shoplifting and then on to a bit of light burgling, you need a few tools.'

'That's Sam's bag,' says her father. 'I've seen him with it.'

'Sherlock Holmes rides again,' says Ella. 'Sam's given it to me to use at home as he doesn't want it any more. All the boys take plastic carrier bags to school, really stupid, but it's the done thing in the sixth form, at the moment. Really dopey, if you ask me . . .'

Her father stops doing the toast and is all attention. He is so rarely told anything about his daughter's life in school, yet here some little titbit is coming out without even being prompted. Ella is immediately annoyed by his obvious interest, which she knows is unfair, but that's how she feels.

'That egg will be rock hard,' she says. 'You know she likes it three-and-a-half minutes.'

'Oh no,' says her father, turning the water off.

'Anyway all those eggs are bad for you,' says Ella. 'Too much cholesterol.'

'We don't have no cholesterol in this house,' says her father.

'Two affirmatives make a negative,' says Ella, then wonders if she's got it wrong. She did get a B in English, which pleased her, though she hadn't done as well as Jules, with an A. Then she regrets trying to be clever, as her father did leave school at fifteen and has never sat an exam in his life.

'Dad,' she shouts after him, as he goes upstairs with the tray. 'Don't turn the water off when you go out. I might want a bath when I get back from, from, being out . . .'

It's on the tip of her tongue to tell him where she is going. If only because it would give him such pleasure.

The same morning, over in Colette's home

Colette and her mother live in a small flat in a large Edwardian house. It's in a quiet road, where nearly all the houses are split into rented flats, mostly fairly worn and crumbling.

Colette is taking a cup of tea to her mother, who is still in bed, still half asleep.

'Get me my cigarettes from the kitchen, darling,' says her mother. 'It is so lovely being looked after.'

'No, I won't,' answers Colette. 'You promised you'd give them up.'

'I can't, I can't. What other pleasures have I got in life?'

'Oh Gawd,' says Colette. 'Not that joke. You have too many pleasures, if you ask me.' She is wondering where her mother went last night, and about the two empty wine bottles she has already put in the bin.

'I've seen your Dimmy smoke,' says her mother. 'So why don't you stop *him*?'

'Mother! He's not called Dimmy. I'll scream if you call him that again,' says Colette. 'And he's not "my" Dimmy either.'

'Sorry, darling,' says her mother. 'Lovely tea. How about a little biscuit?'

'No, you're too fat,' says Colette.

'Don't say it. I know. I should take some exercise.'

'Anyway, I've finished them,' says Colette. 'So you'd better get some more today when you go shopping. Is that clear? And some chocolate as well. There's nothing in this rotten flat.'

'I think you should take some exercise as well, darling,' says her mother. 'Don't they have PT in the sixth form?'

'What are you talking about?'

'Physical Training,' her mother replies. 'Oh they've changed all the names since I was in the sixth form. What's this empathy thing I read about in the *Guardian* the other day?'

'You tell me, Mother,' says Colette. 'You're the clever one.'

Her mother has a degree and dearly wants Colette to follow suit and go to some university, get a career rather than a husband. She never had a real career herself, getting married straight from college. Now, years later, having become unmarried, she works as personal assistant to a production director.

'Where are you going to this morning, anyway?' she asks.

'Out,' answers Colette, going into her bedroom, next door to her mother's.

'That's nice, dear,' says her mother, turning over the pages of the *Guardian*. 'With Dimmy?'

She looks up as she hears Colette give a scream from the bedroom. 'Sorry,' says her mother, quickly. 'Just slipped out.'

'You are so stupid,' says Colette, packing a towel in a bag. 'I really think you are going soft in the head. I don't know how you ever passed any exam.'

'Very true. It does surprise me sometimes. By the way, have you done that essay? Don't you think you should do it this morning, get it over with, hmm?'

'No,' says Colette. 'I'm probably never going to do it. All a waste of time, going to some stupid university. I'm just waiting for some rich bloke to come along, then I'll be off, out of this dump, out of this country.'

'That will be nice, dear,' says her mother. She knows that Colette says it to annoy. 'Do send me a postcard.'

'No, I'll probably never contact you again,' says Colette. 'You'll have to read about me in the newspapers, when I marry for the fifth time, probably some lord or millionaire con man, old enough to be my father. Though Gawd knows how old he is,' she mutters to herself.

Colette's father is never talked about. Last heard of in America; last mentioned by her mother a year ago. It pains her too much to talk about him.

Colette picks up her bag and goes into her mother's bedroom and leans over the bed. 'See you, fatty,' she says, giving her a kiss. 'Love you, poo face.'

Colette goes downstairs, half-wishing she had told her mother where she is going. There is no need to keep it secret; her mother would be very pleased. But there would be one problem. She would want to come as well.

Raffy: ready to serve

EPISODE 4

Still Saturday. A very busy, very crowded, very overstocked but rather understaffed newsagent's shop in St Andrews Road

Raffy is behind the shop counter, imagining he's at the London Palladium, top of the bill, playing to the audience. This is just his Saturday-morning job, so he might as well make it as amusing for himself as possible.

'Right, who's next to be serviced?' he says, clapping his hands, smirking at a woman of about forty at the head of the queue, then rolling his eyes. 'What can I do for you?'

'Just *The Times Lit. Sup.*,' she says frostily.

'That's all you want, is it, darling?' says Raffy. 'Nothing else I can do for you, hmm?'

'No thanks.'

'Actually,' says Raffy, putting on an exaggerated confidential whisper, 'it is rather boring this week, apart from page three. They've got a topless photo of Christopher Isherwood. Very saucy. I'm keeping it on the top shelf in case any impressionable young GCSE students see it . . .'

The woman is not at all amused, but Raffy is, laughing at his own wit. He then turns to two young mums with babies in pushchairs. 'What's your pleasure, darlings?' he leers. 'Me, I hope.'

'*Woman's Own*,' says one of them.

'That's me, darling,' says Raffy. 'I keep myself for women only. That's why we always have a long queue, but I am trying to work my way through them all. Next please.'

There are in fact two long queues, leading to two tills. The other till is being run by Mona, the full-time assistant. Raffy has not noticed that his queue is now headed by Mr Banks, Deputy Head. He has obviously been listening to all Raffy's chat.

'Good morning, sir,' says Raffy. 'Your usual? Now remind me, is it *Spanking Monthly* you get? Or *Rubber Times*? I think we've got one left. Under the counter of course. Say no more . . .'

Mr Banks is holding a *Daily Telegraph*. He looks straight through Raffy, hands over his money to Mona, then walks out.

'What you got on this morning, Mona?' asks

Raffy, pretending to sniff her. 'You're attracting them like flies.'

Mona is a short, heavily made-up, bleached blonde of thirty-five. She tries to treat Raffy like the schoolboy he is, but if she's in the right mood, she can be amused by his cheek.

'You're stupid, you are,' she says. 'One of these days, somebody's going to report you to Mr Patel.'

Mr Patel, the shop manager, sits most of the time in a little office at the back, endlessly putting figures through an old-fashioned calculator.

'Can I put this up?' asks a thick-set man in a dark suit and well-polished shoes.

'This is a newsagent's, sir, not a knocking shop.'

'Knock knock shop?' says the man, confused. Mona smiles. Raffy sighs and takes from the man's hand a piece of type-written paper.

'20p a week,' he says, reading it, 'or 50p for a month.'

He walks to the shop window. Outside is a Jaguar, its engine running.

'"Receptionist Wanted for Health Clinic",' so Raffy reads. '"Must be fit, healthy and attractive. £150 a week." Hey, I might apply for this.'

'It's for a girl,' says the man, handing over the money. 'Stupid boy.'

'Good job you don't say so. Sex Discrimination Act. Not that it bothers me. Where sex is concerned, I have no discrimination. But they could have you, under the Act. Even during the act. That's why we have to check all ads going in the window . . .'

The man has not been listening. He gets into the Jaguar and drives off.

'Nasty bit of work that,' Raffy says to Mona, back at the till. 'Who's next for shaving?'

The queue is soon dealt with. Raffy is about to settle down and read some magazines when he sees that Mr Patel has gone to the front window to study the adverts.

'Cheeky sod,' says Raffy, 'doesn't believe I checked them.' Quickly, he goes into the back office, picks up the phone and dials a number.

'Er, is Taz there, please? . . . No, just say a very good friend of hers.'

Raffy holds on, tapping his fingers, doing a few complicated drum rolls, trying hard to look casual, but at the same time watching Mr Patel's silhouette through the office window.

'What?' says Raffy. 'Look this has got to stop. There was a shortfall of *Sun*s this morning when I marked them up. Someone is nicking them, and it must be at your end, squire. I hope I won't have to tell you again.'

Just in time, he has seen Mr Patel returning. Raffy hangs up, and gives him an obsequious smile. Staff are not supposed to use the phone for personal purposes. Even on work matters, calls must be checked with Mr Patel first.

'You can go now,' says Mr Patel, returning to his desk. 'And I won't charge you for the call.'

'Bloody hell,' says Raffy to Mona. 'He does this every week, one minute before twelve o'clock, so he doesn't have to pay another hour. Oh well, I can go to the match now.'

He gets his bomber jacket and slings it over his arm. As he leaves, Mona beckons towards him. She puts three bars of chocolate into his hand.

'Thanks, Mona,' says Raffy. 'I'll slip you something one day soon.'

Outside, Raffy puts the bars of chocolate in his jacket pocket, alongside the four already there. It's always the same. On the rare occasion Mona is kind to him, it's the day he's managed to nick something anyway.

'Mean buggers,' he says, 'all of them.' Then he gets on his bike and cycles off.

Camden Lock, the Saturday market stalls

Sam, fed up, is sitting behind a stall. He is fed up because this is his father's Saturday stall, which Sam has been forced to look after for a few hours while his father is away buying further junk. Sam considers it all junk, though his father calls it 'ephemera'.

His father's hobby is buying old magazines, memorabilia, shop bills, letter heads, stamps, postcards, books, records and other assorted daftnesses. He has taken the stall in order to try and sell some of his swaps.

'Got any Wembley material?' says a man in an old raincoat.

'No,' grunts Sam. He has no idea what the man means by Wembley material, but doesn't care. He feels cold and is convinced flu is coming on, all thanks to his father.

'Would you like to buy some *Health and Efficiency*?' asks another man in a shabby raincoat, this time carrying an old, battered suitcase.

'I could do with some,' says Sam. 'I'm probably about to die.'

The man opens the case and starts to take out some tattered magazines. Sam stares at them, quite interested by some of the old-fashioned photographs, then the man starts spreading them all out, covering the stall.

'No thanks,' he says, quickly. 'We're not buying today, thank you.'

Another old man stands for ages, examining everything on the stall, turning stuff over and holding things up. 'Oh, if I had a penny for all of these I threw away,' he says. 'Goodness, I remember these. But they should have a stamp at the bottom. Look, no stamp, see, the stamp's missing, no stamp.'

'Yes,' says Sam wearily. 'I can see. No stamp. You're right.' The man shoves the card right under Sam's nose, blowing on it, and shooting dust into Sam's face, along with a generous portion of his own germs. Sam stands up and starts coughing and spluttering, till at last the man moves away.

So far this morning, he has sold very little, just a few first-day covers to children for 50p each. He knows for a fact his father paid a lot more for them.

At this rate, sales will not cover the cost of the stall, never mind Sam's wages, which are supposed to be £2 an hour.

Sam looks under the stall at a box of old clothes his mother has given him and takes out an ancient sports jacket of his father's. His mother has been clearing out his father's old clothes, without telling him. Sam puts on the jacket to keep warm, though it is too big and just hangs on him.

Almost immediately, someone comes up and admires it, a young and elegant woman. It is Taz.

'How much?' she asks. She recognizes Sam, though she is not sure of his name. She does manage a quick smile.

'Er, I dunno,' he mutters. 'What do you think?'

'Would £20 be all right? That's what they cost in Covent Garden.'

'Fine,' says Sam.

Taz disappears into the crowd for a moment, and Sam can just see her talking to some man in a suit, who appears to be getting out a wallet. She then reappears with the £20. Sam is well pleased. It means the cost of the stall has now been covered. He looks in the clothes' box and pulls out another tweed jacket. This time he puts it on the stall, priced £20, then finds a Fair Isle pullover to keep himself warm.

'Any *Beatles Monthlys*?' asks a voice. It is Ken Grott, sixth-form tutor and man of the people.

'There might be one in that box.'

'Don't you know what you've got?' says Mr Grott.

'Nope,' Sam answers. 'It's my dad's stall.'

Mr Grott finds a *Monthly*, marked at £2.50, which Sam says he can have for £2. 'I'm feeling generous today,' says Sam. 'I hope I'll get a good essay mark for that.'

'I'm always generous,' says Mr Grott. 'But some people are never going to get good marks. How much for the pullover?' He offers £5, which Sam accepts at once. 'Got any more sixties clothes?'

Sam is not aware that they were from the sixties, he just thought they were old clothes, but he points to the box. Mr Grott quickly rakes through, pulling out a kipper tie, for which he offers £1. He admires the tweed jacket, but says he can't afford it.

'I'll come back next week,' he says. 'See what you've got.'

By twelve o'clock, Sam has sold all the clothes except for one pair of flared trousers, though several people examined them and one girl even tried them on. As for the ephemera, no more of it has been sold.

Just after twelve, Sam's sister Sarah arrives to take over the stall, moaning and groaning. She has no interest in running it either. Sam shows her where the float is, but takes the big money with him. He intends to keep most of it, as his mother gave him the old clothes to sell.

'Here we go, here we go, here we go,' shouts a voice. 'Ar-sen-al, Ar-sen-al, Ar-sen-al.' Then there's a lot of clapping, one-person clapping, which sounds a bit thin. It is Raffy, come to pick up Sam.

'Hope you got some money,' says Raffy. 'That sod never paid me today.'

'Loads of money,' says Sam.

'That's good. You can buy my ticket. I'll buy the chocolates . . .'

Later, outside a semi-detached 1930s suburban house

'Bloody hell,' says Raffy. 'I expected something a bit grander than this, for somebody who went to Westminster.'

'He probably got a scholarship,' replies Sam.

'I think I would have stayed there, if I'd been him,' says Raffy. ''Stead of coming to our dump.'

'He'd heard about you, Raf,' says Sam. 'That was the big attraction.'

'*One* of the attractions,' says Raffy. 'He's really come to take an A level in Legover. None of that at these boys' public schools. It's each man for himself there, or each other, if they're pretty enough . . .'

They ring the front-door bell and a foreign au pair answers. At once, Raffy is all charm, trying to be an English gentleman. 'I say, my dear little mademoiselle, is Toby at home, hmm? You know, Toby, as in Shakespeare?'

The girl looks totally confused. Raffy stands back on the steps, holds his arms out and starts declaiming.

'To be, or not to be,' he shouts. 'Gerrit, eh?'

The girl closes the door.

'I think she's Swedish,' says Sam.

They wait for a few minutes on the steps, then Toby himself appears. He is wearing a red-and-white Arsenal scarf and hat. That's the first thing which strikes them. No one over the age of twelve wears their favours to football matches, not if they want to stay un-thumped, un-molested.

'But we are going to see Arsenal,' says Toby, puzzled by their expression. 'Surely that's all right? I wouldn't wear Arsenal colours if we were going to White Hart Lane, would I?'

'You've got a lot to learn, sunny Jim,' says Raffy.

Raffy's face has become strangely contorted, and he is trying desperately hard to contain himself. Sam is also trying hard not to burst out laughing. They have both suddenly noticed something else about Toby, now that he has unwound his scarf and taken off his Arsenal–Celtic pom-pom hat.

'Everything okay?' Toby asks, slightly bemused.

'No problems,' says Raffy, grinning. 'I've got the chocolates.'

'Where's Dim?' says Toby. 'I thought he was coming.'

'He works all day Saturday,' answers Sam. 'And most of the night as well.'

'And Jules, is he working?' Toby asks.

'Shopping,' Sam replies. 'I suppose that's work of a sort. That's all Jules does every Saturday.'

'And what about the girls? I mean, women.'

'Oh they're not coming,' says Raffy. 'Just as well.

What would Kirsty say . . . ?' At that, he can contain himself no longer. He lies down on the pavement and rolls about with laughter.

Toby, dear Toby, after just one week in his comprehensive sixth form, has made a big decision. That morning, he has had his hair done. In dread-locks. Toby, gentle Toby, has become a White Rasta . . .

Ella: naturally fit

EPISODE 5

Meanwhile, in an Institute in darkest Camden Town, several women are sweating violently

An all-women weight-training session is now in progress. Among the heaving, panting bodies are Ella, Kirsty and Colette. They are by far the youngest in the room. Most of the other women are much older, around thirty, and a lot heftier and more out of condition than these three.

'I'm knackered,' moans Colette. 'Can't we have a rest?'

She is sitting astride a sort of rowing machine where she has been for some time, though the instructor has advised them to use each machine in turn, for thirty seconds only.

'What you trying to do anyway?' shouts Kirsty.

'Fat thighs,' groans Colette.

'You've already got them.'

'Ha bloody ha,' says Colette.

Kirsty comes across. She alters the mechanism for Colette, changing the weight control, and points out which levers and pulleys to push and pull to get the maximum benefit for thighs.

'Inside or outside?' she asks.

'Don't care,' says Colette. 'Just get rid of these bleedin' thighs for me. Then I can have a break, and some chocolate . . .'

Kirsty returns to her machine for the required time, following the right exercise to tone her back muscles. She gets up to thirty-five kilos, her best so far.

Ella is also doing well, zooming with ease round the circuit. She looks very athletic, in her skin-tight black cycling shorts, just like Kirsty's. Both she and Kirsty are naturally fit and athletic. In the first year, they both played netball for the school. In the second year, they both ran cross-country for the school. In the third year, *nada*, *rien*, nothing at all. That was it. Goodbye all physical exercise. Hello boys.

Ella's father was particularly upset. He used to go jogging with his daughter, playing tennis and swimming too, and he had fantasies of her running for Camden, or London, if not England.

Colette, who has always been clumsy and uncoordinated, was quite pleased when the others gave up games. She had felt out of it for a couple of years, even though she tried to mock them for being hearties and sporties. So she liked it when they became almost ashamed of ever having played games, denying any interest, scheming to get out of PE and even bunking off on occasions.

'I don't think I'm getting any thinner,' moans Colette.

'How many times have we got to tell you?' says Ella. 'That's not the point.'

'And I certainly don't want any horrible muscles,' says Colette.

'That's not the point either,' says Kirsty.

'Don't tell me, luvvy,' says Colette, giving up. 'It's to raise my consciousness. Well I don't want it raised. I like it lying flat.'

'Don't we all,' says Kirsty. They all laugh, a girls-together, locker-room laugh.

In the showers, more perspiring females, including Kirsty, Colette and Ella

'Isn't it funny,' whispers Kirsty, 'how the really ugly, fat, horrible ones prance around showing us their all. Look at her. Ugh!'

'Are you talking about me, you poo?' says Colette.

'Don't be stupid,' says Ella. 'You know you're not fat. But you do eat too many sweets. You should cut down, just for the sake of your health.'

'I know,' says Colette. 'But I can't stop.'

'Well at least this will help you,' says Ella. 'I think we should come every week from now on. Keep you fit, toned up, in condition. Burn off some of the gunge.'

'Are you going out tonight, Kirst?' asks Colette.

'Well I'm not staying at bleedin' home, am I?' says Kirsty. 'In that dump, with my shitty family.'

'So where you going?' asks Colette.

'Dunno,' says Kirsty. 'I don't want to go out with that flash pig. In fact I'm fed up, pig sick. With everything. And everyone.'

'Hey,' says Colette. 'I thought you were the one trying to persuade me how good all this horrible exercise is for you, toning up your mind and your consciousness, and all that crap. Hasn't done you much good, sister . . .'

Outside the Institute. The three girls emerge, hair still a bit wet, but very clean and healthy-looking.

'What shall us do now?' asks Colette, as they stand on the pavement.

'I dunno,' says Kirsty. 'Don't care.'

'I know,' says Colette. 'Let's have a milkshake.'

'Wash your mouth out,' says Ella. 'What a disgusting suggestion.'

'How gross,' Kirsty says. 'After all that exercise. It'll ruin the good of it.'

'Right,' says Colette. 'Glad you all agree.'

'My treat,' says Kirsty. 'My brother gave me some money.'

'You mean the horrible one?' says Ella.

'They're all horrible.'

They set off, arm in arm, taking up the whole pavement. A Jaguar practically runs into them, coming to a halt not far from the Institute, its tyres half on the pavement. There is a chauffeur in a suit at the wheel.

'Bloody cheeky sod,' shouts Colette. 'Watch what you're doing with that load of scrap metal, mate.'

'Up your bum,' shouts Kirsty.

The driver ignores them, jumping out and rushing to open the back door of the car. Out of it steps Taz, in a designer tracksuit.

She strides past them, only recognizing them at the last moment. Pausing for a fleeting moment, she gives them a quick 'Hi', then goes inside.

'Stuck-up bitch,' Colette says.

'Lucky beggar, if you ask me,' says Kirsty.

They walk slowly along the road, thinking about Taz. Behind them, another weight trainer comes out of a side turning. She is an older woman, in a very cheap and ill-fitting Woolworth's pink track-suit and carrying two Marks and Spencer carrier bags, full of food. She doesn't see the girls. She stops outside the Institute, examining the notices and times for the women-only sessions.

'Oh my God,' screams Colette, who has turned round, just to see if the Jaguar is still there. She grabs Kirsty and Ella by the arm.

'Let's run,' she says. 'It's my mum . . .'

An intimate, discreet, tasteful corner of a select but very popular eating rendezvous. It's called McDonald's.

Colette is slurping her milkshake. She feels it is justified, after expending all that energy. She is also eating french fries. They have ordered two large portions between the three of them, but so far Colette has managed to eat most.

'Imagine if she'd come in while we were there,' says Colette. 'I would have died.'

'Well at least your mother gets herself out of the house,' says Kirsty. 'Mine just sticks at home all day in the kitchen, like a flamin' martyr.'

'I think she's a good sport, your mother,' says Ella to Colette, watching the french fries disappear.

'You sound like Toby,' says Colette. '"Good Sport", what, what.'

'I think he's lovely,' says Kirsty.

'We know,' says Ella. 'You've told us.'

'I've got his address,' says Kirsty. 'Raffy gave it to me. Let's go and see him, eh?'

'Oh yeah, great idea,' says Colette, sarcastically. 'Get ourselves invited in, for sherry and canapies.'

'What's them?' asks Kirsty.

'I dunno. Except you put them over your head when it rains.'

'I don't wanna go home anyway,' says Kirsty. 'I hate home. I'm thinking of leaving.'

'Where you going?' asks Ella.

'Dunno,' says Kirsty. 'Perhaps to Toby's. Stay in his west wing, or the servants' quarters. Either that or a squat.'

'Hey, look,' says Colette. 'See what I can see?'

'Not Taz again,' says Ella.

'Don't say it's your mother,' Kirsty says. 'Come to guzzle, just like her daughter.'

'No, the next table,' says Colette. 'Look . . .'

Ella and Kirsty turn round, but there is no one at the next table. All they can see is a pile of the usual leftovers, spoils of the lunchtime war, greasy paper still oozing with obscene gunge, torn napkins stained blood-red with ketchup, the carcasses of dead cardboard boxes.

'So what's all the excitement?' Ella asks.

Colette is on her feet, looking round carefully, just in case the previous customers might come back. Then she makes a grab for some uneaten french fries, hidden under the debris, which only she has spotted.

As she is about to touch them, a uniformed arm gets there first. One of the staff is clearing the table, distracted, mind miles away, mechanically going about her business.

Colette pulls away, embarrassed to be caught, then recognizes the waitress, a girl from the fifth year whom she has never liked.

'Get your rotten hands off,' she growls, taking the french fries. 'Don't you know sixth formers have priority?'

'What a pig you are,' says Ella. 'How can you eat other people's food?'

'Easy peasy,' says Colette, sitting down again. 'Just open zee mouth and in eet all goze, *comme ça* . . .'

At the bus stop, three girls at rest, waiting, waiting

'I'm going to buy a car,' says Kirsty.

'What with?' asks Colette, eating one of her stolen chips. 'Persil coupons?'

'It's the first thing I'll do,' says Kirsty, 'when I get a job.'

'And when will that be?' asks Colette.

'Soon, pretty soon, just as soon as I can manage it,' says Kirsty. 'I hate having no money. Hate having to get handouts from my lousy brothers. They've always got lots of money, and they're stupid and lazy and pigs.'

'Those are the people who make money today,' says Ella. 'But they're doing boring jobs, and in the end they'll grow to hate them. So it's better to hang on, and try to get a reasonably interesting job.'

'You sound like Mr Witting,' says Colette, 'doing his twitting.'

'The thing is,' Kirsty goes on, 'I can't think of what I want to do. And if I did, I wouldn't get the qualifications anyway.'

'You will,' says Ella. 'I'm sure you will, if you want to.'

'But I don't want to,' says Kirsty. 'I can't face two years' work in the sixth form, and three years at some potty little college on some stupid course, if I'm lucky. Then what? That's five years lost. I'll be an old woman by then. I want to be enjoying myself, *now*.'

'You mean like working in McDonald's,' says Ella. 'Really good fun that.'

'Sounds great to me,' says Colette. 'In fact I think I'll go back for another milkshake. I'm ravenous, just standing –'

Ella and Kirsty each grab her by a shoulder and march her in the opposite direction. They have decided to walk home, as there is still no sign of a bus.

A little later, on the way home

'Hello, darling,' shouts a voice.

Kirsty, Colette and Ella stop and look around. Two young workmen, high up on the scaffolding of a house, are whistling and shouting at them. They are stripped to the waist, showing off their tattoos.

'Give us a bit then,' yells one of the men, seeing Colette finishing off the last of her chips.

'I could give her a bit,' says the other. 'Oooh.' He makes an obscene gesture with his arms, then gyrates his body.

'What do you think of this, darling?' yells the other, pretending to unzip his trousers.

'Just ignore it,' says Ella. 'That's the only way to deal with them.'

'Piss off,' says Kirsty, but not too loudly.

'Up your bum,' adds Colette.

'I told you not to,' says Ella. 'It just encourages them.'

The girls walk on a few yards, with Ella trying to make them walk more quickly.

'I bet that fat one's a goer,' shouts the first workman. 'I bet she likes a Big Mac.'

The two workers yell some more, pouring out further filth and four-letter words, much to their own amusement.

'Get stuffed,' shouts Kirsty, rather loudly this time.

'Oh yes please,' both men answer.

'Let's see what *you've* got then,' yells Colette. She stops and goes back to the house. Ella is still wanting them to move on.

'Show us what *you're* so proud of,' shouts Kirsty. She joins Colette, both of them standing at the bottom of the scaffolding. 'I bet he hasn't got anything,' says Colette. 'Just a big mouth.'

'He looks tasty, though,' yells Kirsty. 'The little weedy one on the left. I prefer a little one myself.'

'Ooh, give me the one with the big bum,' leers Colette. 'I do like a big bum.'

'Yeah,' says Kirsty. 'Let's see your bum then.'

'I bet they're both right goers,' says Colette. 'How long can you manage, darling, three seconds or four seconds?'

Colette and Kirsty both give dirty laughs. Ella has now stopped and joined them. The two young workmen are rather taken aback at this reversal, by the two girls answering back, and can't think of what to say in reply.

'Come on, lover boys,' yells Colette. 'Don't be shy.'

'We won't laugh,' says Kirsty. 'Not much.'

'It's all gone quiet over there,' sings Colette, copying the football chant.

'I think they're just a couple of plonkers,' says Kirsty. 'What a disappointment.'

'Piss off, scrubbers,' yells one of the workmen, but not as raucously as before. They have both disappeared from sight, inside a window.

'Come on, Ella,' says Kirsty. 'Let's get them.' She puts down her bag on the ground, takes off her jacket and rolls up her sleeves. Ella looks puzzled for a moment, then she does the same. Both of them jump on the first rungs of the scaffolding, yelling and shouting as they start swinging.

Colette, not one of nature's gymnasts, yells out a commentary, encouraging them upwards and onwards. 'Are you ready, lads?' she shouts. 'Gerrem off. Here they come. It's your big chance. Can you manage it? Are you up to it? Now we'll see what you're made of! Now we'll see who's a goer . . .'

Not a sound can be heard from the two workmen. They are somewhere deep inside the house, out of sight. Ella and Kirsty stop climbing when they reach the first floor, but still continue their shouting. They wait, smiling, give a final few yells, then drop lightly down to the ground, easily, athletically. All three girls go off, arm in arm.

'They can't help it, poor things,' says Ella. 'It's

their conditioning. You've got to feel sorry for their tiny brains.'

'See?' says Colette. 'That's what happens when sisters fight back.'

'Sixth-form sisters,' says Ella, putting her arm round Kirsty, 'should stick together . . .'

And so, singing and chanting, the three girls return home.

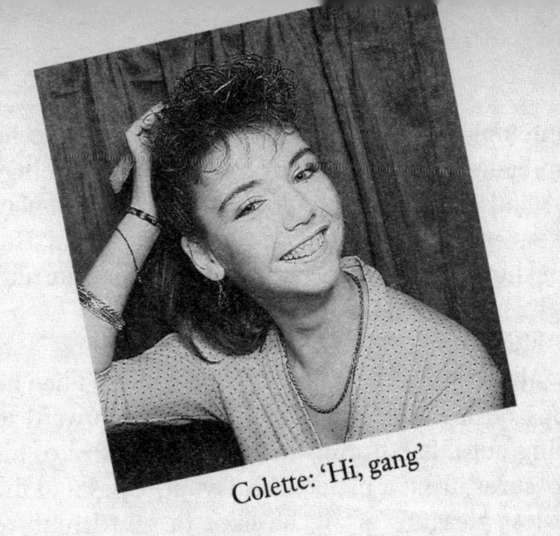
Colette: 'Hi, gang'

EPISODE 6

Saturday night, Sam's house, about eight o'clock

Ella and Sam are in Sam's bedroom, on the top floor of the house. There is an air of quiet expectation, subdued excitement. After all, it is Saturday night. Who knows what fun lies ahead.

Sam has just had a shower, so he looks clean and glowing. He is standing in his boxer shorts, a present from Ella, wondering what to put on, which ensemble to stun the Saturday-night world with. He looks around at his clothes strewn on the floor, and can't decide, so he goes across and gives Ella a cuddle.

Ella is standing in front of the mirror, brushing her hair, then tying it up. She pauses for a moment, contemplating the effect, allowing her body to be cuddled. She is in her best Saturday-night going-out clothes, though deep down, she does not want to go out at all. She wants to stay in, just with Sam. But she knows he has made arrangements for Saturday night, as all good boyfriends should.

'Hurry up,' says Ella. 'It's getting late.'

'Always time for a cuddle,' Sam replies. Then he flops on his bed, sighs. He is looking forward to going out this Saturday night, but like most of his pleasures, from a plate of his favourite pasta to the bestest pleasure of all, he likes to spin it out, to savour it.

Sam puts on another reggae record and picks up that afternoon's Arsenal programme, wishing he had not gone. He has compromised his principles. As a true Spurs supporter, he should have stayed away, but he wanted to see Spurs' deadliest rivals get beaten. They won, while Spurs, playing away to Liverpool, got thrashed. That's another reason for going out – to forget.

'Where we going then?' asks Ella.

'Out, of course,' says Sam.

'Did you get the tickets for Dingwalls?'

'I dunno,' says Sam. 'Dim was supposed to get them.'

'Dim?' says Ella.

'That's what Raffy said.'

'Raffy?'

'You haven't got a lot of conversation tonight, have you?' says Sam. 'Hey, listen to this bit, really good.' He turns the volume up. The sound of banging comes through from the ceiling below. It is his father, complaining about the noise, so he turns it down, marginally.

'But I thought it was just you and me going?' says Ella.

'Yeah, well, Raffy and Dim wanna go as well, and Toby, so we might as well all go together, seems sensible. Hey, did I tell you about his hair? He's got dreadlocks! Raffy took the piss out of him something rotten. I bet he'll go and wash them out . . .'

There is loud shouting from downstairs. Sam's father, sounding very bad-tempered, is calling Sam's name, but the sound of the music drowns his words. The bedroom door opens and in comes Raffy, all cocky, clapping his hands and chanting 'Arsenal, Arsenal, Arsenal.' He lights a cigarette. Ella opens the window and glares at him.

'Thanks, darling,' says Raffy. 'I like a big ashtray.' Sam starts to get dressed, still undecided. In the end, he puts on what he'd already taken off. At least he is clean underneath. And his trainers have had an airing for a couple of hours.

Raffy is wandering round the bedroom, looking through Sam's records and tapes, then his copies of *Dandy*, *Beano* and *Shoot*, all kept in the wardrobe. That's why his clothes are always strewn round the room, or spilling out of drawers.

'Wish I had a room of my own,' says Raffy. 'Wish I had a home.'

'I wish you'd sit down and shurrup,' says Ella.

'Oh temper, temper,' says Raffy. 'Take it out on him, not me.'

There is more shouting from downstairs, as Sam's father is forced once again to answer the front door. This time it is Kirsty and Colette arriving.

'Hi, gang,' says Colette. 'Anything to drink, anything to eat?'

'Go and make it,' says Sam. 'You know how.'

Sam's friends have been coming to his house for years. It is a big house, compared with the others', and as he lives nearest to the school it has always been a calling point. His mother has encouraged his friends to come; his father has never been quite so keen.

Colette declines to go down to the kitchen, having seen Sam's father's face at the door.

'It's a lovely room you've got, Sam,' says Kirsty. 'Why don't you look after it better? It's so scruffy. If I had my own room, I'd decorate and paint it and have it really good.'

'Have you got the tickets then, Sam?' asks Colette.

'Dim's getting them,' he replies.

'No he's not,' says Colette. 'He's not going. He's working all night.'

'Don't worry,' says Raffy. He goes to the bedroom door, opens it and pulls in the telephone from the landing. It is an upstairs extension, meant to be shared between Sam and his sister Sarah, meant to save Sam's father from shouting up the stairs every time one of them is wanted on the phone. Raffy makes several calls, arrangements and counter-arrangements, where to meet, who to meet, what to do.

Times passes. More records are played, more calls made, more moans at Raffy. Friends ring back, suggesting other arrangements, which leads to arguments amongst everyone. The plan eventually alters. They are all now going to go to the Town and Country Club, not to Dingwalls, to listen to a new reggae band.

'Okay,' says Sam. 'I'll go and make coffee. Who wants some?'

Raffy turns the music up higher as soon as Sam leaves the room. Ella tells him to turn it down. More arguments. Kirsty and Colette are going through an old photograph album of Sam as a little boy, shouting and shrieking. Then they find some primary school photos, in which most of them appear. More shouting and shrieking.

'Look, are we going out or not?' says Ella. 'I'm fed up hanging around here.'

The phone rings. A friend in their tutor group tells them all the tickets for the reggae band are sold.

'I don't think I'll go out,' says Sam, returning. 'It's too late. I feel knackered already.'

'On Saturday night?' asks Raffy. 'Everyone goes out. It's a rule of nature.'

'I know, let's all go to the pub,' says Kirsty.

'Yeah!' says Colette, putting on the excitement.

'How pathetic,' says Ella.

They all get up, turn the music off, open the bedroom window even wider to let the fug out, then troop down the stairs.

'Thank God,' says Sam's father to Sam's mother. He is sitting in their living room on the first floor, but his voice can be clearly heard. 'It's been like a bloody herd of elephants up there for the last two hours.'

They all make faces on the landing. Raffy gives a V-sign. Colette and Kirsty giggle. On the ground floor they meet Sarah, coming out of the kitchen in her pyjamas, carrying a mug of cocoa.

'Lucky beggars,' she says, going up the stairs past them. 'Wish I was going out to have a good time.'

Still Saturday, the night still young, ten o'clock at the Dome bar in Hampstead

They are standing on the pavement, outside a very popular French-style bar. It is impossible to get inside for the jam-packed crowd. It is almost impossible to stand on the pavement for the overspill, most of it overdressed, overloud, overexcited.

'God I hate this place,' says Ella. 'I didn't want to come.'

'Look, we couldn't go to the Bull again,' says Raffy, swigging from a bottle of German beer. 'We go there all the time. This is Saturday night.'

'If you say that again,' says Ella, 'I'll scream.'

'You're just a poser, Raffy,' says Kirsty. 'That's why you like it here.'

'No he's not,' says Colette. 'He just poses as a poser. He hasn't got the style.'

'Haven't got the money, you mean,' says Raffy. 'Hey, I wonder if Jules is here. Or anyone else.'

Raffy stands on tiptoes, hoping to catch sight of someone he would like to see.

'Jules wouldn't come here,' says Kirsty. 'He knows it's full of phoneys. Nor would Taz. She's got more taste.'

'Toby might be here,' says Colette. 'Except they probably wouldn't let him in. He only looks thirteen.'

'I don't think they'd even let him in Mothercare,' says Raffy. 'Did I tell you I started boozing at thirteen? And since then, I've never been asked my age.'

'Were you born with a seven o'clock shadow, Raffy?' asks Colette, all bright eyes. 'Do tell.'

'The thing about starting early,' says Raffy, 'is that I can hold my drink, unlike some people I could mention.' He looks straight into Sam's eyes.

Sam turns away and tells the girls about Toby's new hairstyle, describing it in great detail. Raffy butts in, wanting to tell the story himself. They push and shove each other, laughing and shouting, competing for attention. The girls scream and laugh at the description, wanting every detail.

Time passes. They each have several more drinks, especially Raffy. Even Ella is beginning to enjoy herself. 'Poor Toby,' she says.

'He's so sweet,' Kirsty says.

'I think he's lovely,' says Colette.

'Hey, *Toby*,' Raffy shouts. 'We're over here, old chap.'

Raffy is pretending he has seen him through the crowds, pointing inside the bar, putting on a posh voice. They all follow his gaze, till eventually they realize he has been kidding.

Together, they jump on Raffy, in fun of course, shrieking and shouting, grabbing his drink from him. He yells back, pushing and shoving the others, who in turn are also pushing and shoving, yelling and shouting. All of them, even our heroes, are overexcited and overloud, even the ones not overdressed.

Raffy gives a groan and rushes to the edge of the pavement. He is quietly, almost sedately, sick.

Midnight, or thereabouts, at a bus stop

'Bye, darling,' says Kirsty, giving Colette a kiss as she gets on the bus.

'See you,' says Raffy.

'Are you sure you'll be okay?' Kirsty asks Colette.

'What about me?' Raffy says. 'No one ever asks me that.'

'Of course,' says Colette. 'Don't be a poo.'

The bus draws away, leaving Kirsty and Raffy on the pavement. Sam and Ella have already gone home, walking in another direction.

'We should have gone with Colette,' says Kirsty. 'Seen her home.'

'Give over,' Raffy replies. 'I'm knackered. Any way, she'll be okay. She does it all the time.'

'Yes, I know, but Saturday night . . . Those late-night buses are full of drunken yobs. Such as you. How do you feel now anyway?'

'Getting better,' says Raffy, putting on a drunken lurch, though he is still unsteady. 'Here, give us a kiss.'

Kirsty pushes him away, but she does allow him to put his arm round her. They walk in silence.

'Her mother will probably be out when she gets home,' says Kirsty. 'She hates going into that empty house. I should have gone home with her, stayed the night.'

'Gawd, give us a break.'

'Well you should at least have offered to see her home.'

'I'm taking you home,' says Raffy. 'That's bad enough. Then I'll go home on my own, in my condition. You feminist girls never seem to worry about boys walking home on their own. I've seen the figures. Most muggings and beatings-up on the street happen to blokes.'

'But you're so brave, Raffy.'

'What you worried about anyway, with all your muscles? I thought your weight-lifting was supposed to make you super-strong.'

'Weight-training,' says Kirsty. 'It's not the same thing.'

'Let's have a feel anyway,' says Raffy, grabbing her. 'Hmm, t'rific pectorals, Kirst.'

'Gerroff,' Kirsty replies.

'How did it go this morning anyway?'

They are now arm in arm again. Kirsty tells him about her morning, what exercises they did, how Colette's mum arrived just as they were leaving. Raffy tells her about his morning in the shop, the customers who came in, such as Mr Banks, and the advert going up.

'Oh yeah,' says Kirsty, remembering what she'd meant to tell him. 'After we'd finished this flash Jag turned up, and out gets Taz, thinking she looks like Lady Di.'

Raffy is stopped in his tracks. He wants more details, the car described, the driver and what he was wearing.

'She really does fancy herself,' says Kirsty.

'And I fancy her as well,' says Raffy.

'What a pig you are.'

They have now reached Kirsty's block of flats. Raffy tries to pull her into one of the concrete garages, mostly unused for fear of vandalism and filled with junk.

'Just a quick cuddle,' says Raffy.

'Get lost,' shrieks Kirsty. 'I thought you were ill. Just try that one more time and I'll –'

'Scream,' suggests Raffy, holding her against a wall. 'They scream all night round here. It's normal.'

'I'll get Kevin.'

'Oh, got me really scared now,' says Raffy, still not letting her go.

'Okay then,' Kirsty tells him. 'We'll go upstairs to the end of our landing.'

She takes his hand, looks around, and they walk into the block towards the lift. Just as the lift comes, Kirsty lifts up her foot, Karate-style, and kicks out at Raffy, pushing him away. She jumps into the lift and its doors slam in Raffy's face. 'Good job I did that special leg-muscles exercise today,' she thinks as the lift takes her up. 'It's come in rather handy.'

Sam's house, also around midnight

Sam and Ella are coming through the front door, trying to be absolutely silent, but Sam is having trouble taking his key out of the front door. They shush each other, then giggle.

'Just a quick coffee,' whispers Sam, pulling her in. 'Then I'll take you home.'

'My dad will go mad,' says Ella. 'It's so late.'

'Can't you say you're staying at Colette's?'

'Not now. I told them I'd be back.'

They creep up the stairs, making a face at every creak from the floorboards, making extra faces as they pass Sam's parents' bedroom.

On the door of Sam's room is a note in Sarah's handwriting. 'Where is my Beatles tape? I want it NOW. Horrible.' They start giggling again. The door has to be pushed slightly, as it has never fitted, and they both fall inside. Sam pulls Ella on to the bed beside him.

'Where's the coffee, then?' she says.

'Youfacoffee?' asks Sam.

'That's an old one,' Ella groans. 'I don't think even Raffy would use that.'

'You know he got the best marks yesterday from Old Banks. People are always surprised to find he is clever. And from Banko too.'

'Pity he wasn't kinder to Kirsty,' says Ella. 'He's got it in for her.'

Sam can think of a Raffy-like response, but says nothing. They lie for a while, side by side, saying nothing, then Sam gently puts his arms round her. After a while, they move together, carefully. They lie in this position for some time, fully dressed. 'My arm's gone to sleep,' says Ella.

'Shush, wake up arm,' says Sam, kissing her arm, then her lips.

'No really, Sam, don't. I'll have to go. This is silly.'

'Seems very sensible to me,' Sam says. 'Logical in fact. Nice evening, nice people, nice times.'

'Hmm,' says Ella. 'You don't know my dad.'

'Funny. Could have sworn I was introduced to him. Don't say that was your lodger was it? Bloke with a taxi?'

Ella smiles, and when Sam puts his hand on her leg, she does not resist. They lie in silence again. After a while there is a tap on the bedroom door, a pause, then another tap. Sarah's voice can be heard, under the door, asking for her Beatles tape, this moment, she needs it *now* for her project. 'Get to bed,' shouts Sam, angrily. 'Don't be such a pain.'

Ella smiles. It takes some time for Sam to return to his former position and the possibilities it offers. Eventually he does.

'SAM!'

This time it is his father's voice. There follows a banging on the ceiling from a walking stick, which Sam's father has acquired especially for this purpose. 'What time do you call this!'

Slowly, Sam removes himself from Ella, then from his bed, gets up and puts his shoes on. They go downstairs and Sam walks Ella home.

'I don't know why people think it's so marvellous having your own room,' he says. 'You can have your own room in prison.'

Kirsty: leaving home

EPISODE 7

One week later, Kirsty's home, eight thirty in the morning

'Kirsten! Don't you know what time it is?'

Kirsty's mother is standing at the kitchen stove, as ever, shouting to her elder daughter.

'You'll be late for school. Get up at once.'

Kirsty turns over, opens half an eye and sees that the other bed is empty. Mandy, her younger sister, has already gone to school. Her two brothers and her father have left for work ages ago. She turns over again, facing the wall, and closes both eyes.

'Kirsten! If I have to tell you one more time!'

Her mother is now standing over Kirsty, shaking

her till she opens an eye again, the other eye this time. She lies thinking, trying to work out where she is, what that wall is doing there, who chose that horrible wallpaper, what day it is, why she has opened alternate eyes. Weight-training for eyes. She smiles. Why not? They need exercise, just like any other part of the body. She decides to tell Colette this idea at school today, it will amuse her. Then she remembers what day it is. What she has decided to do today.

'Thanks, Mum,' she grunts, heaving herself up.

Her mother has brought her a mug of tea, still with her pinny on, still looking harassed although the breakfast pandemonium is over for the day. She should be able to relax, take it easy till the next shift, but of course she won't. Life for her is just one long shift. Kirsty is determined to make sure that does not happen to her.

'I shouldn't do this,' says her mother. 'It's not helping you.'

'Mum, you just spoil everyone,' says Kirsty. 'That's your role in life. Then you'll go to heaven, and live happily every after. Or do you "live" in heaven? Isn't it just sort of stationary, like death, only warmed up . . . ?'

'It's too early in the morning for that sort of talk,' her mother answers. 'Now please get up, there's a good girl. You know I worry about you being late.'

'Mum, I've told you. My first lesson is a free period. I don't have to be in till ten o'clock.'

'Oh,' says her mother, relieved. Then she pauses, just as she is about to leave the bedroom. 'Aren't you supposed to spend your free periods in the common room or the library?'

'Who told you that?' says Kirsty, knowing she never did, as she makes a point of not telling her mother or any of her family anything about school. It's all too boring, and anyway they would not understand. Perhaps Ella has been talking to her, or Raffy, just to stir things up.

'I think I read it,' says her mother. 'In one of those sixth-form leaflets you brought home.'

'Yeah, well, you can work at home, or in the common room or library. You didn't read it properly.'

'Seems a funny place, this sixth form,' says her mother. 'Sounds like Liberty Hall to me.'

'Might sound like it,' says Kirsty, 'but it's not. It's more like an open prison. You think you're free, but they're on at you all the time, moaning and hassling you.'

'Good, that's what you need,' says her mother, going to the bedroom door.

'Oh, Mum,' Kirsty says, sweetly. 'One other little thing.'

'Yes, dear?'

'Could you just see your way to turning on Capital? Thanks.'

Her mother goes back to the bedside and switches on Kirsty's radio. 'What did your last maid die of?' she asks.

'Overwork.'

'Well that won't happen to you,' says her mother.

'You'd be surprised,' says Kirsty, supping her tea, listening to her radio.

School, second lesson of the morning

Ken Grott is sitting with his feet up on a desk. Around him a group of lower sixth formers, members of his Sociology class, are also lolling with their feet up.

'It's the fault of society,' says Toby. 'You have to blame the Tories, for turning this country into a materialistic, non-caring society.' Toby now has short hair, very short. He washed out his attempt at dreadlocks, then had it all cut off.

'So what have the Tories got to do with it?' Raffy asks.

'It's thanks to them,' Toby replies, 'that these people are left out, the deprived and unemployed with no educational qualifications, so naturally they behave like hooligans.'

'I like the use of the word "naturally" there, Toby,' says Mr Grott. 'You might have hit on something. Perhaps it is "natural" to behave the way they do?'

'Cobblers,' Raffy says. 'I've read all that shit as well. Typical of academics. If they can go back in history and prove it's all happened before, that we've always had people behaving like hooligans, then they think that means you need do nothing about it.'

The subject under discussion is Football Violence, causes and cures thereof. Raffy has usually taken the lead in most of these class discussions over the years, always willing to shoot his mouth off and not worrying about being embarrassed or proved wrong, but the arrival of Toby has given him some strong opposition.

'These people are failures in their ordinary lives,' continues Toby. 'Football hooliganism is their only chance to give themselves an identity.'

'What do you know about football hooligans?' Raffy says. 'Most of them have got jobs; they're all well-dressed. Shows how much you know.'

'But you can still be deprived,' says Toby, 'spiritually.'

'Bloody hell,' Raffy says. 'We've got the Archbishop of Canterbury here this morning. Let us all pray for the souls of the poor football fans . . .'

'So what is your explanation, Raphael?' asks Mr Grott.

'First of all, it's a laugh, it's good fun,' Raffy replies, 'fighting and shouting, going on the rampage. Secondly, it's nothing to do with the Tories or class. It's classless. Happens in all parts of society. Look at those rowing people at Oxford, those drunken Etonians you read about. They're all the same. Just that the yobs don't get away with it the way the yuppies do.'

'That's true,' says Ella.

'I was talking,' says Raffy, not giving Ella a chance to continue or any of the other girls time to join in. 'I remember in the third year when we were on that German trip, all of us got drunk and then went round trying to wreck caffs, shouting and swearing at Germans, looking for a fight. We were all saying "We won the war." It was good fun, a laugh.'

'So do you think patriotism comes into it?' says Mr Grott. 'It's all just jingoism?'

'I think you have a point there, sir,' says Toby, 'I mean Ken. If you read the *Sun*, as I do every day, you'll see this revolting anti-foreign thing all the time, pandering to our worst motives, stirring things up.'

'Okay then, clever guts,' Raffy jumps in. 'How do you explain, say, Chelsea versus Millwall fans, eh? They're the worst, but they're not foreigners.'

'In a sense they are,' says Mr Grott. 'But I think you have a good point there, Raffy. It could help to explain why English fans are worse than those of other countries. That seems to be true, according to the media. Why, I wonder?'

'It's cos we're an island,' says Raffy. 'Brought up to hate foreigners.'

'I never thought of that,' Toby allows, making a note in his file.

'Do you think there are any environmental causes?' asks Mr Grott. 'We don't care for our surroundings any more, so we don't care about other people either?'

'Yeah, I do,' says Raffy. 'Our estate is disgusting. That's why the Tories are doing the right thing – are you listening, Toby? If they make us all into house owners, we'll look after our surroundings better.'

'Not all community housing gets wrecked,' says Toby.

'Here we go again,' Raffy answers him. 'You just don't know, do you. Mine is a dump, so is Kirsty's. In fact hers is worse, like a bloody bomb site.'

'Is that true, Kirsty?' Mr Grott asks, looking round. 'If so, do you think there's a relationship, cause and effect, hmm?' There is no reply.

'She's not here today,' says Ella. 'I don't know where she is.'

Meanwhile, Kirsty's flat

Kirsty is leaving home, stepping carefully over the debris as she gets out of the lift. She is looking rather smart, wearing a black skirt, not too tight, and a white blouse with a black tie, loosely knotted.

'Perhaps I should have put on my tracksuit and looked healthy and fit,' so she thinks to herself. 'Hmm. I always feel comfortable in that. This blouse is killing me. I think that Mandy's been wearing it. Pig. Wait till I see her tonight. If I see her. If I come home. Be good if I don't . . .'

Kirsty turns down the main road, away from the direction of school, walking quickly. She is in good time, but is undecided about the best route to take.

'Oh Gawd, I've left the *A to Z* at home. And I put it by my bedside last night. Mum's fault. She must have moved it. Typical.'

She reaches Camden Town, trying to remember which side street will be the quickest short cut, and then exactly which mews she is looking for.

'I'll be doing this route every day from now on. Won't that be funny? I'll see the same people, same things, same shops being opened up at the same time every day.'

She pauses, trying to remember the street names.

'That's if I come this way. I wonder if there's a bus. Oh bloody hell, look at that, a dirty mark on my blouse already.'

She stops, tries to wet it with spit and wipe it off, but only makes it worse. Readjusting her tie so it covers the mark, she smiles and walks on.

'It's Mum's fault. She's got no sense of direction either. Funny how it runs in families. Raffy is brilliant. Goes somewhere once and never forgets the way. Perhaps I need specs. Perhaps I've done too much eye-training. What am I doing. I'm not thinking of Raffy ever again.'

She stops at a corner, near a newsagent's kiosk.

'Should I get a paper. Will I have time to read it. Will it be go, go, go all day long. I know, I'll get *The Times*. That will look good. Impress the boss and the customers. Or the *Guardian*, as old rot-guts Grotty is always telling us. Bugger him. He'll be showing off now, trying to get Ella and Col to join in his phoney discussions. What a plonker. All of them. Especially Raffy. Bugger them all. I'll buy the *Express*. I only like reading the *Express* anyway.'

Kirsty stops at the kiosk, but does not buy a newspaper: the ink might come off on her blouse. Instead, she asks the newsvendor for directions.

She has been to this mews place once for her interview the week before, and felt sure she would recognize it again. This morning everything seems strange.

'Mews' is a rather grandiose description for what is little more than a yard leading to a converted warehouse, entered through an old brick arch. Most of the houses are empty, but no doubt they'll soon be gentrified, like so many in the surrounding streets.

The name of the establishment Kirsty is looking for is also rather grandiose. Even Kirsty, with her poor sense of direction, knows she is still in the heart of Camden Town. Yet 'Regents Park Fitness Club', says the brass plaque beside the discreet entrance. The windows are black, giving nothing away, and there is an entry-phone system by the door.

'Strictily Membrs Only', reads a handwritten note, rather scruffy, which has been sellotaped to the door.

'Hmm, someone didn't get GCSE English. Well, that's something I did achieve in my school life, all those years ago . . .'

Kirsty presses the bell. She stands and waits, ready to give her name, ready to start her first ever day at work.

Dim: money matters

EPISODE 8

Next day, sixth-form common room, lunch hour

They are all sitting around. Most people are eating and chatting, but a few are eating and reading. The eating mainly consists of crisps, sandwiches, hamburgers, salads. Colette is on cakes and chocolate. Most are also drinking – Perrier, Coke, sugar-free orange juice. Raffy is on beer, swigging from a large can. It is strictly against school rules to drink on the premises during school time, even for sixth-form members.

'I wonder why Banko was looking for Kirsty this morning?' says Colette.

'That stupid probation thing, I suppose,' says Ella.

'Did you go and see her last night?' says Colette.

'No, I was going to, but I had my essay to do. I rang her though. Her mother said she was out.'

'I don't know what you're all fussing about,' says Raffy. 'You never worry about me when I have a day off.'

'No one worries about you,' says Colette, 'full stop.'

'Toby does,' says Raffy, throwing his empty beer can in a corner. 'He's never come across anyone like me, but then he hasn't been many places, have you Tobe?'

Ella gets up, rather sanctimoniously picks up the beer can and returns it to Raffy. 'You get rid of it,' she says, quietly. 'If it's found in here and Banks is told, you know what will happen. We'll *all* have to suffer, not just you.'

Raffy looks at her for a moment, half sneering, as if he is about to throw it back at her. Everyone watches.

Sam stops reading *Smash Hits*, wondering what is going to happen. If Raffy is horrible to Ella, what will he do? Will he have to take her side and thump Raffy, or should he just get up now and say he's going to the bogs?

Raffy stands up, smiles, bows before Ella, and proceeds to squash the can flat, very slowly, holding it in one hand, as if performing an amazing feat of strength. 'Sorry, your Majesty,' he smirks, finally putting the can in his pocket. 'And sorry it took me so long. I know you girls – sorry, women –

can squash cans in seconds, thanks to that weight-lifting.'

They all ignore him, knowing he wants someone to correct him so that he can make some equally smart remark.

'As for squashing things between your muscular thighs,' adds Raffy, going to the door, 'wow. I'm really terrified.'

'Get out, pig,' says Ella.

'In fact every bloke is terrified,' says Raffy, standing with the door open. 'You'd better watch out, Tobe. If one of them captures you, and they're all sniffing around, be jolly careful. They're like bloody Amazons . . .'

'Piss off,' says Colette, throwing an empty Mr Kipling cake packet at him.

'Good riddance,' says Ella, as Raffy goes out.

All of them, without knowing why, feel instinctively that Kirsty's absence is somehow to do with Raffy.

Through the door comes Jules, like one of the characters on a Swiss cuckoo clock, swinging into view as the other disappears. Mr Nasty goes out; Mr Nice comes in. 'I've rung her,' he says.

'And what happened, luvvy?' says Colette, jumping up. All of them look towards him, wanting to know if he has found out anything.

'I got her mum,' says Jules.

'And what did she say?' asks Ella.

'She said Kirsty was at school,' says Jules. 'Seemed surprised I should be ringing.'

Episode 8

Regents Park Fitness Club

The lunchtime rush is over. Kirsty, the new receptionist, has been booking in businessmen all through the lunch hour and early afternoon, but now there is a lull. She sits at a white leather reception desk with three white telephones, on a white chair, surrounded by a small ocean of white fluffy carpet. Kirsty has never been in such a luxurious establishment before.

'Everything okay, Kirsten?' asks a posh voice from a side office. It is Mrs Scott-Scott, who can see Kirsty through the one-way glass mirror on her office door, as well as looking at her on the video screen which monitors everyone in the club. Yesterday it gave Kirsty quite a fright when she realized she was being observed.

Most of yesterday they sat at the reception desk together, as Mrs Scott-Scott showed her what to do. Kirsty found it a bit confusing at first, with so much to do and often all at the same time, but by the evening she felt she'd got the hang of it.

Today, Kirsty is in sole charge of the reception desk. First, she has to handle all calls and fill in the appointments book. Then she has to greet the members as they arrive, being as charming and polite as possible. Mrs Scott-Scott insists on that. She has to check them in, making sure they sign the members' book, and give their full membership number. She then has to give them a towel and a dressing gown, and send them to the appropriate area: sauna, massage, relaxation therapy, whatever it is they want. Most just have a massage. If they request a particular masseuse, Kirsty has to make sure no cubicle or masseuse is double-booked.

'Do you think you've got the hang of it now?'

'Yes thanks, Mrs Scott-Scott,' says Kirsty.

Mrs Scott-Scott insists on her full name, but Kirsty hopes that she will be allowed to drop that eventually.

'Good,' says Mrs Scott-Scott. 'I thought you coped very well yesterday. I can see a big future for you here, my dear.'

'That's nice,' says Kirsty, wondering what Mrs Scott-Scott might have in mind. She has hardly seen the masseuses yet, apart from glimpsing them arriving for work. So far they have all gone straight to their own cubicles at the rear of the building. One of them, very tall and fit-looking, came in a fur coat today. This impressed Kirsty, as do all the framed certificates on the wall, listing their numerous qualifications, many of them from organizations abroad.

'Which way would you look to go, Kirsten my dear?' asks Mrs Scott-Scott.

'How do you mean?' says Kirsty. It feels a bit eerie, carrying on this conversation with someone she can't see.

'Well it will all be up to you. Whatever you fancy, really. It will be in your hands.'

'Sorry?' says Kirsty.

'Well, you could become a masseuse yourself.

You do look the part. I mean, I know you're terribly keen on keep-fit. I'm not quite sure though about the weight-lifting . . .'

'Weight-training.'

'Sorry, weight-training. We like our girls to be fit, but, you know, to keep themselves feminine.'

Kirsty decides to ignore this. Mrs Scott-Scott is pretty old, probably fifty, and can hardly be expected to understand modern aerobic methods. She has already seen the club's so-called gym, which is hardly bigger than Kirsty's bedroom, and contains only coconut matting, some wall bars and a vaulting horse.

'Of course you would have to pass all the tests,' continues Mrs Scott-Scott.

'Yeah, well,' says Kirsty. 'I thought I'd finished with all those exams when I left school.'

'Oh I'm sure you'll pass them,' says Mrs Scott-Scott. 'It's just common sense. We can fix that. We'll get you through. Or you could go up the management ladder. We have other establishments, and from time to time I have to visit them, so I will be needing a good deputy manager some day, some time. We shall see.'

'I'd be interested in that,' says Kirsty.

'Good,' says Mrs Scott-Scott, tottering out of her office on her high heels, her body jangling with all her gold bangles and necklaces. 'Just popping out for a moment. Hold the fort, will you?'

Kirsty waits a few moments, still watching the

one-way glass in case it's a trick, and Mrs Scott-Scott has somehow come in again. Then she gets up and pops her head into the office, taking a quick glance, just to make sure. There is no one there. All she can see is a small video monitor, trained on the empty gym.

'Hello,' says Kirsty, in her best receptionist's voice. She is now back at her desk, speaking on the telephone. 'Is that the School Secretary? Good, it's Kirsten's mother here, Mrs Connolly. Yes, speaking. I'm afraid Kirsten is ill, very poorly; we've had the doctor but he doesn't know what it is. She'll be off all week. Thanks for calling. I mean, thanks for taking the message. Have a nice day . . .'

Friday night, at the Cow and Bull pub

Colette, Raffy, Ella, Toby, Jules and Dim are sitting in a corner, drinking half pints as it's only Friday and they're only poor sixth formers.

'Perhaps she's been abducted,' says Colette. 'Drugged and beaten and taken to South America.'

'Lucky beggar,' says Raffy. 'I fancy that. Where do you book?'

'Ken Grott says she's ill,' Jules says. 'He's had a message from her mum.'

'Oh, that explains it,' says Ella. 'I rang twice and got her brothers and they just said she was too tired to talk.'

'I wonder if she'll come to weight-training tomorrow,' says Colette.

'Not if she's ill,' says Ella.

'I think I might be ill,' Colette says. 'I haven't recovered from last week.'

'Oh no, you agreed,' says Ella. 'Every week from now on.'

'My theory is she's run away,' says Toby.

'What do you know about her?' Raffy asks.

'She seemed pretty fed-up all last week.'

'She's always fed-up and moaning. That's her style. You don't know her.'

'I wonder where she would run away to,' says Jules. 'Perhaps we should alert the police at Carlisle station, or Newcastle, or Glasgow . . .'

'What are you on about, Jules?' says Colette.

'When provincial kids run away, they're always found hanging about Euston station or Kings Cross. So we should do the opposite. Nobody would think of looking for a runaway London kid up there.'

'She hasn't run away,' says Ella. 'She's too sensible.'

'Yeah, but she does hate her family,' says Colette.

'That's normal,' Raffy says. 'If I had a family, I'd hate them. That's what families are for. You can't hate yourself.'

'Some people do, Raffy,' says Jules. 'Not everyone has a high self-image, like you.'

'I think most people hate something about themselves,' says Ella. 'Often something stupid.'

'There was one kid, at my old school,' says Toby, 'who committed suicide after his A levels. He thought he'd failed. Then when the results came out, he'd got three As.'

'Oh God, this is becoming morbid,' says Colette. 'Who's having another drink?'

'Me,' says Raffy. 'As long as someone else is paying.'

'Don't look at me,' says Dim.

'Oh you are lovely,' says Jules. 'Don't be selfish. Let's look, let's all feast our eyes on him.'

They all turn and look lovingly at Dim. He has been reading a copy of *The Financial Times* which he has found at the bar, studying the shares, taking no notice of the conversation so far. 'No chance,' he says. 'I've got no dosh on me. It's all tied up.'

Dim is known for his knowledge of money matters and the care he takes with his own. He usually has some cash in his pocket, even on a Friday. No one else has any more money, not that they're letting on about, so they all sit, spinning out the dregs in their glasses.

'Perhaps she's running away from school, not her family,' says Toby. 'It wouldn't surprise me.'

'Here he goes again,' says Raffy. 'Hardly been here three weeks, and he thinks he knows it all.'

'You mean she's just staying at home?' says Ella.

'Bunking off, we call it,' says Raffy. 'Do you want me to write it down for you, Tobias?'

'Thanks, Raf,' says Toby. 'Perhaps you could help me with the letters. I can't do joined-up writing yet.'

'Good one, Tobe,' says Colette.

'Yes, you really have had a deprived education so far,' says Raffy, sarcastically.

'How do you mean?' asks Sam.

'Well he comes here,' says Raffy, 'ponces into our sixth form, just to take advantage of our good times.'

'But how's he deprived?' asks Ella.

'What he's been deprived of,' says Raffy, 'is what we had to put up with in the third and fourth years. Two years learning bugger all. Chaos in every class. Kids wrecking the joint.'

'That was you, Raf,' says Sam. 'You were the worst trouble-maker in the third year.'

'Exactly,' says Raf. 'That was a learning process in itself; learning how to survive in a comprehensive. If you struggle through that, you'll get through anything.'

'It's true,' says Toby, quietly. 'I've missed the worst in a sense, and come for the best. But it's not my fault. I didn't want to go to Westminster. It's taken me all this time to get out of it, to realize I hated being with one social class, one sort of ability. It's so elitist. It's expected you'll be trying for Oxbridge; if you're not capable, or not interested, you don't get the same attention. I wish I'd been with mixed-ability groups all the way through. You're the lucky ones.'

'Thanks, Toby,' says Raffy. 'Cheers. Have a drink.'

Raffy empties his already empty glass. They all sit silently. It's the first time that Toby has explained his reasons for coming into their sixth form.

'Well, if everyone is too mean to buy me a drink,' says Raffy, 'I'm going.'

They all start to get up. As they do so, the pub door opens and in comes Kirsty, all smiles. 'Drinks all round, you guys,' she says. 'Come on, what you having? Whiskies, vodkas, name your poison.'

They stare at her for a moment, as if hardly able to understand, then Kirsty opens her purse and flashes a bundle of notes, £150 worth. 'I've had my first pay,' she says. 'One hundred and fifty smackeroos. So let's celebrate.'

They all crowd round her, pushing and shoving, asking her questions. She refuses to explain anything till each one has ordered and the drinks are in.

'So what's happened?' asks Ella. 'We thought you were ill.'

'I've left school,' says Kirsty. 'That's all. But don't tell my mum. I'm not letting her know at the moment, till I move out.'

'You what!' exclaims Colette. 'Where, when, how?'

'I've seen this little flat in Kentish Town, well just a studio thing really, one room, £60 a week rent. But I've got to pay a deposit of £100, plus four weeks' rent in advance. It'll only take me three weeks to earn that. No problem. Loads of money. Crisps anyone? Peanuts, pork scratchings? You like them, Raffy, being a pig . . .'

'What's the job then, Kirsty?' asks Jules.

'Confidential,' says Kirsty. 'I'm not allowed to tell. It's a private establishment, very exclusive. I'm about to be made assistant manager, after only one week. Amazing, isn't it.'

'Do you enjoy it?' asks Ella.

'Brilliant,' says Kirsty. 'Really good. And I love the money.' She waves her wad of notes again.

'If it's £150 a week,' says Dim slowly, 'that's £450 for three weeks, but they'll take off tax, probably emergency tax at the top rate, plus your National Insurance. So you'll end up with only £300, in cash.' They all listen, amazed at this long speech. 'I'd wait six weeks if I were you, Kirst,' adds Dim.

'Whatja mean?' says Kirsty, waving her money again. 'It's all cash; there ain't nuffink taken off. It's all cash-in-hand business. None of that tax non-sense. This is an exclusive, high-class place.'

'Sounds weird to me,' says Toby, looking worried.

'You haven't been around enough,' says Kirsty. 'And it was all thanks to Raffy I got it. Come on Raf, double whisky, old son?'

'Me?' says Raffy, looking puzzled. 'I didn't do anything.'

'That's what they all say,' says Kirsty, laughing.

In a week, her laugh does seem to have become more raucous. They all look at her, half-jealous, half-worried.

Raffy: street encounter

EPISODE 9

Regents Park Fitness Club, one week later

It is mid-afternoon. At this time of day, things are rather quiet in the health and massage world. After the first flush of learning a new job, Kirsty is beginning to find the days slightly repetitious. She has also found herself being asked to stay on later and later in the evening. And some of the customers are beginning to be a trifle familiar with her, especially the regular ones. She is becoming increasingly suspicious.

The front-door buzzer goes and Kirsty picks up the intercom phone. 'Yes?' she says. Her instructions are to wait until the member gives his name or number before letting him in.

'Hello, sexy,' says the voice. 'It's Fumf here.'

'Who?' She vaguely recognizes the posh accent.

'Colonel Fumf.'

'Oh, you.'

Kirsty lets him in. It is Colonel Ronny, a very regular customer: large, florid and distinguished. He is dressed in a pin-striped suit and a blue shirt with a white collar. He comes most afternoons about four, straight from some West End club for officers and gentlemen, or so he has told Kirsty.

'And how are you today, my dear?' he asks, beaming at her, perhaps more florid than usual after his lunch.

'Fine thank you, sir,' says Kirsty, smiling a glazed smile which she has managed to perfect in just two weeks. 'And how are you, Colonel?'

'Ready for my usual workout,' he beams. 'Unless there's anything un-usual on offer, har har har.'

'We do try our best,' says Kirsty blankly.

'Actually, I think I'll try Marlene today. She does have a nice personal touch, hor hor hor.'

''Fraid she's off, sir,' says Kirsty. 'She's rung in sick, got some infection.'

'What?' For a moment the Colonel looks a bit worried.

'A flu bug, I think,' says Kirsty. 'There's a lot of it around.'

'Oh, I see. What about Natasha? Is she free?'

'Occupied,' says Kirsty. 'But you could wait. Or go into the gym for a warm-up session first.'

'Gym? What gym? Oh, that place. I'm not the type

to hang from wall bars, though I do have my little ways, as you must have heard by now, ha ha ha.'

'Felicity is free,' says Kirsty, looking down her list, ignoring his jokes, 'and Ramona. Would you like her, or someone else?'

'What about you, my dear? Are you free, hmm? Or terribly expensive, hee hee.'

'I'm not a trained masseuse, sir.'

'All the better, my dear. We can learn together.'

'Sorry about that, sir,' says Kirsty, writing his name in the book, then getting out a towel and dressing gown and handing them to him. 'I'm sure you'll be happy with Patience. She's in cubicle four. Thank you, sir.'

'I'm not at all happy,' says the Colonel, suddenly looking very bad-tempered. 'Not happy at all. Where's Scotty? After all the years I've been coming here . . . I am an account customer, you know. I've introduced a lot of very important people to this establishment.'

The phone rings and Kirsty picks it up. The Colonel, still grumbling and grunting, takes his towel and goes through the louvred doors to the cubicles, crashing the doors on their hinges as he slams them open.

Mrs Scott-Scott comes out of her office, once the Colonel has gone in, and waits for Kirsty to finish taking a booking on the phone.

'Kirsty,' she says, 'you've still got a teensy weensy bit to learn here, I'm afraid. You haven't quite got the hang of things yet, have you?'

'Oh yes I have,' says Kirsty.

'Not quite. For a start, never say one of our girls is ill, certainly not with an infection.'

Kirsty realizes that Mrs Scott-Scott must have been watching, and listening, on the closed-circuit video.

'That's what Joan told me on the phone,' she says.

Kirsty only discovered yesterday that Marlene is really Joan, that Natasha is Doreen, and that all the girls have professional names. Mrs Scott-Scott explained to her that it was for convenience, as each little cubicle has the name of a masseuse on front. It saves repainting when they leave.

'I don't care what she told you,' says Mrs Scott-Scott. 'You either say a girl is occupied, or gone to Paris for a special training assignment.'

'How could she?' says Kirsty. 'Joan's feller would kill her. He's on the phone all day long, moaning about having to look after her kids. I bet that's why she's off, if you ask me . . .'

'Don't argue with me, child,' says Mrs Scott-Scott. 'Just do what I say. And if you want a future in this establishment, you'd better be prepared to do what customers ask you to do.'

'No chance,' says Kirsty. 'I'm not a trained masseuse.'

'We can call you a trainee, if you insist,' says Mrs Scott-Scott. 'Don't be so stupid and naive.'

Being told she is naive and stupid makes Kirsty feel she is back at school again.

'And if you want to earn real money,' adds Mrs

Scott-Scott, 'that's where it lies. You can double your salary in tips alone if you're willing to please customers. It's up to you. Am I making myself clear . . . ?'

Outside school. End of another day.

Raffy is in his shades, waiting for someone. He has on a new yellow Walkman, bought with his Saturday-morning earnings.

'See you, Raf,' says Sam, walking past arm in arm with Ella.

'See you, man,' says Raffy, clicking his fingers.

'Waiting for some girl, eh?' Sam asks, stopping and turning round.

'Woman,' says Ella to Sam. 'I've told you. It's demeaning to refer to any female over puberty as a girl. And it's more offensive to use the word "lady". We are all women.'

'Hard luck, Sam,' shouts Raffy after them. 'You tell him, Ella, keep him in hand. Know what I mean, say no more.'

'I like your Walkman,' says Sam, realizing Raffy has bought a new one, very expensive, usable under water.

'Walkperson,' yells Raffy. 'Do get it right, dum dum.'

Sam and Ella disappear, still holding hands. Raffy checks his watch, looks back toward school, then goes out into the main road, just in case.

'Taz!'

He has suddenly seen her, coming out of the side entrance which the caretaker usually locks.

'It's me,' shouts Raffy, catching up with her and falling into her stride.

'I know who it is,' says Taz, very cool.

'Oh rapture!' exclaims Raffy. 'She knows who I am. I do exist. My living has not been in vain.'

'That's a matter of opinion.'

'Oooh, clever stuff, keep little Raffy in his place, keep him panting, which I am of course, completely out of breath with all that running, but still got lots to offer, such as a helping hand for women in distress, note the use of "women" not "girls", "girls" should only apply to females pre-puberty, oooh, 'scuse my French . . .' Raffy is rabitting on, hoping to get a smile. No luck so far, Raf. Keep trying.

'So can I help you carry your Gucci school bag? Must be awfully heavy. Or your Rolex ruler? I know, what about your Hermes homework? I can come round to your place and help you with it. You've probably heard I'm the cleverest person in the whole school.'

'Yes,' says Taz. 'You've told me.'

'Curses,' says Raffy. 'I can never keep secrets. Can I ask you something very personal, hmm?' He jumps in front of her, stopping her walking. She stares through him, but there is by now perhaps the merest trace of a smile on her face.

'What are you doing tomorrow?' asks Raffy. 'Saturday.'

'Yes, I do know it's Saturday,' says Taz. 'We have a calendar at home.'

Raffy smiles at this. Almost up to his standard. She gently pushes him aside and walks on, followed by Raffy.

'So what about it?' he says.

'I thought you were always busy on Saturday,' says Taz. 'Working in the shop.'

Raffy stops. He never for one moment believed she would know anything about him at all.

'After that, you'll be going out with Kirsty, won't you?' says Taz. 'You're still friends, are you? After all, I gather you helped to get her the job.'

'You what?' says Raffy. 'Nobody knows what her job is. She won't tell anyone.'

'Oh I see,' says Taz. 'But don't you work in that newsagent's?'

'Yeah,' says Raffy.

'It's one of my father's, actually,' says Taz. 'Think about it.'

They have turned down a side street. A Jaguar is waiting, engine running, chauffeur at the wheel. Taz jumps in and the car drives away. Raffy is left still trying to work out what she has told him.

Regents Park Fitness Club. Next day, early afternoon.

Kirsty is returning from her lunch break. She has had to take it rather late, as there was a sudden rush of customers. While she has been away, Mrs Scott-Scott has been looking after reception.

'Nice lunch I trust,' says Mrs Scott-Scott, glancing at her watch.

'Lovely, thanks,' says Kirsty. 'I went into the park. Didn't realize it was so far away.'

'Perhaps you shouldn't go so far,' says Mrs Scott-Scott. 'Perhaps you should stay here and have sandwiches, as the girls do.'

'You mean ciggies,' says Kirsty. 'That's all they seem to live on. I like to keep healthy, know what I mean.' Kirsty smiles; it is after all supposed to be a health club. Mrs Scott-Scott does not appear to see the joke.

'Anyway, thanks for manning the desk,' says Kirsty. 'I mean womaning. Or should it be "personing"? In our sixth form, Ella, that's ma friend, tells people off if they get it wrong, or what she thinks is wrong, what the feminists think is wrong . . .'

'What are you talking about, child?' says Mrs Scott-Scott.

Kirsty takes off her jacket, hangs it up, then sits at her desk. 'Sorry, luvvy,' she says, picking up the appointments book.

'And don't call me "luvvy",' says Mrs Scott-Scott, going back into her own office.

Kirsty thinks about explaining that it's a jokey name which they all use, ironically but affectionately. Originally they were taking the mickey out of people who use such phrases, now it's just become part of their everyday school speech. But it would take too long. Mrs Scott-Scott would never understand.

Kirsty checks the bookings, running her eye down the lists, but finds her mind is running down the number of days since she left school. Hardly three weeks. Seems a lifetime away. She wonders how long it will take to forget the unspoken, easy routines and relationships she has built up over the last five years. Work is fine, well mostly. The money, that's brilliant, and this Friday she'll pay the deposit on the flat. But the lack of friends, that's a drag. It's only now that she is beginning to realize how much she is missing them. And missing the laffs, perhaps most of all.

'I'm just popping out for half an hour,' says Mrs Scott-Scott. 'I have not had my break yet, waiting for you. And I've got to go to the bank. Try to be charming, if that's possible.'

Kirsty flicks a V-sign to her back as she turns round, then looks round guiltily in case she is being watched. But how can she be? The monitor is in Mrs Scott-Scott's office. The office is usually locked when she goes out, as that is where the money is kept, but this time it has been left open. Kirsty decides to look in. Not to find out details about the club, the membership lists, or the money, as she considers all that boring. She wants to see the inside of Mrs Scott-Scott's drawers, just for fun, poke her nose into anything personal, any juicy letters or even just her handbag.

'There must be some gen about the old bat in here,' says Kirsty to herself. 'Something I can get on her.'

The office is dirtier and dustier than she expected, full of filing cabinets, mostly locked, dirty tea cups, out-of-date calendars, and faded photographs of models with their phone numbers scrawled in felt pen. The only high-tech item is the closed-circuit video. The screen flickers away, trained on the reception desk, now of course deserted.

Kirsty stands at the video, idly flicking through the controls, turning the camera first to the gym. Empty as usual, and badly in need of a clean. She turns to Marlene's cubicle, also empty. She is a bit surprised to find every part of the club is linked up, but of course it helps security in case any of the girls should be attacked. They do get some bad-tempered and rather funny customers, as Kirsty has seen.

When she flicks the camera on to the next cubicle she is surprised to find that Natasha, otherwise Doreen, has a customer. 'Hmm, must have come in when I was out,' thinks Kirsty.

She can see a naked man, face down, flat out on a towelled bench. Natasha is standing in the corner, apparently washing her hands, or getting something ready.

'What a flabby bum,' thinks Kirsty. 'He could do with more than a massage. A crash diet more like, and losing a few stone.'

She is about to flick to Patience when she notices that Natasha is taking off her clothes, or some of them. She is now standing in a little apron, like a

French maid, and holding what looks like a stick. The man appears to be cowering, but nothing has happened to him. As he turns over on the bench, Kirsty sees his face for the first time. He looks instantly familiar.

'I know that head, and those ears. Now who the hell is it?' She fiddles with the knobs, trying to zoom in or get a better picture.

'Mr Banks!'

Kirsty is so surprised she almost knocks the screen off the desk. Imagine the Deputy Head being here! Banko, of all people. She watches for a few more minutes, averting her gaze several times, out of modesty, out of disbelief, and once because she's laughing so much, till she sees Natasha putting her ordinary clothes on again.

Kirsty rushes to her desk and sits down, then rushes back, realizing she has left the camera trained on Natasha's cubicle. She switches it back to the reception desk, closes the office door firmly, and returns to her work.

She forces herself to look busy, reading the booking lists. She notices that there is no Mr Banks booked in. Can she have made a mistake? Can the video have tricked her somehow?

The swing doors from the cubicles open and out comes Mr Banks. No doubt about it. It's him, she thinks, then corrects herself. It is he. Jules told her the verb 'to be' takes the first person, whatever that means. She did get a C in English, even if she rarely uses it properly.

Mr Banks goes straight past her, looking neither left nor right, obviously in a great hurry.

'Goodbye, Mr Banks,' Kirsty finds herself saying. She had decided to say nothing to him, to spare his embarrassment, but this is a way of proving who it really is and reassuring herself that she is not dreaming.

'Huh,' says Mr Banks, giving the bossy grunt she knows so well. He looks at her for a second, straight into her face, but says nothing.

When he has gone, Kirsty goes back to the book. Under Natasha for 3.30 the booking says 'Mr Potter'. 'No wonder I didn't notice it,' thinks Kirsty. '"Mr Potter"! He's using the headmistress's name. Cheeky sod . . .'

Toby: a gentleman caller

EPISODE 10

Kirsty's home, Friday morning

It is just after ten o'clock. Kirsty is having her breakfast, tea and cornflakes, while her mother bustles around. Kirsty has told her not to, as she does know how to make tea and she is also capable of pouring out her own cornflakes, but her mother cannot change the habits of a lifetime.

Kirsty says little, trying to be nice, not critical. Today is the day, the Big Day, when she will get her third pay packet and reveal to her mother that she has left school, got a job and is now about to move out into her own place. But somehow, she just can't get round to the right choice of words.

'What was your very first job, Mum?' she asks, propping up the *Daily Express* against the cornflakes packet.

'Oh, I can't remember, dear,' says her mother.

'Oh Mum! You can't remember anything. You don't know what time I was born, what time Kevin was born, or Mandy. You've forgotten our birth weights. All the vital things, you can't remember any of them. I don't think you are my mother after all. Come on, tell me now, the truth, I was adopted.'

Her mother pauses. For a brief moment, Kirsty imagines she might by chance have hit on a secret. She really is adopted, she can now leave home as a free person and spend the rest of her life hunting down her real parents: her father who was a once-famous brain surgeon and her Irish mother, a poor trainee nurse; or could it be he was a Dublin lorry driver and her mother an eminent London QC, and they met when she was defending him when accused of a terrible crime he never committed? Kirsty's mind does tend to race on, given half or even a quarter of a chance.

'I went into service,' says her mother.

'The Army or the RAF? Don't say it was the Royal Navy. Did you know Prince Andrew?'

'I worked for this lady as a maid,' says her mother, ignoring Kirsty's smart remarks, her mind triggered back. 'Well it was all I could get, leaving school at fourteen with no qualifications. You're so lucky, Kirsten, all those GECs you've got, going into the sixth form and that.'

'Oh yeah,' says Kirsty. 'I wouldn't be too sure of that. I don't call it lucky. In fact –'

'And all this work you're doing, all these late nights after school, all this extra tuition, I'm most impressed. You really seem to have knuckled down in the last few weeks . . .'

'Actually, Mum, I've got something to tell you –'

There is a knock at the door. Her mother jumps up and rushes for her purse. 'It'll be the club man,' she says. 'Friday morning, I always forget, now where did I put it? Oh heck.'

'Watch your language, Mother,' says Kirsty. 'This is a God-fearing establishment.'

Kirsty gets up and goes to the door. Standing there, looking very, very young but very determined, is Toby, pulling himself up to his full five feet six inches.

'Hello, Kirsty,' says Toby. 'So how are you?'

'Fine, okay, fine,' says Kirsty, trying to pull the door to behind her so Toby can't get in. Kirsty hates anyone coming to her house, even her girlfriends, and tries hard never to invite them home. As for boys, not one has ever got inside before, not even Raffy.'

'So you've recovered,' says Toby sarcastically.

'What?' says Kirsty, then she remembers the excuse she gave for her absence. 'Oh yeah, much better now, thanks. Was you just passing?'

'Not really,' says Toby, wondering where he could be passing to, at the top of a high-rise tower. 'I just came to see you.'

'Oh that's nice. Well here I am. Fine, as you can see . . .'

'Can I come in?' Toby asks, getting his foot in the door before Kirsty can close it.

'Bring him in,' shouts Kirsty's mother. 'The money is somewhere. Now where the heck have I put it? Won't be a minute . . .'

Toby pushes the door open and goes in.

'I just want to talk to you, for a few moments,' he says.

Kirsty's mother turns, surprised at the voice, so light, so young, so well-educated, not the heavy Glaswegian accent of her club collector. She gives a little jump when she sees Toby.

'Oh, hello,' she says. 'You've come to see Kirsty, have you? Some tea? You'll be wanting some tea. I'll put the kettle on.'

'No thanks, Mrs Connolly,' says Toby. 'I've got to get back. I just have one free period, and we're not supposed to leave school during a free period.'

'Oh, that's funny,' says Mrs Connolly. 'Kirsty says she can leave school any time . . .'

'Well, as she's left school, I suppose –' says Toby, but Kirsty breaks in, grabbing him by the arm and frog-marching him towards her bedroom.

'Thank you, Mother,' says Kirsty, making a face at her. 'That will be all. You're dismissed, back to the kitchen. Remember you are still in service.'

In Kirsty's bedroom, seconds, just seconds later

'I think you're being very silly,' says Toby, sitting on Mandy's bed.

'Who asked you?' says Kirsty.

'Everybody knows you've left. It's all round the sixth form.'

'Oh God. I'll have to tell her now.'

'You never gave the sixth form a chance,' says Toby, 'that's what I don't understand. It really was rather impetuous.'

'No, it wasn't.'

'Everyone felt out of it that first week. It was all so strange. All that Induction stuff. Timetables, masses of paperwork. Nobody liked that. You just have to get through it.'

'No, I didn't mind that,' says Kirsty.

'Raffy then? You fell out with him . . . ?'

'Oh him, he's irrelevant. He always was. Always will be.'

'You were doing so well,' says Toby.

'Rubbish,' says Kirsty.

'But you were,' says Toby. 'In the classes I was in, you had ideas, you took part.'

'Yeah, but speaking's speaking. That's easy. I hate doing those essays and I don't understand nuffink about that Sociology. Grotty thinks I'm stupid; Banko just hates me. All the books are rubbish – you'd fink it was a foreign language. You've got to go along with all that phoney stuff. Turned me off. Well out of that, I can tell you.'

'How are you getting on with your job?' asks Toby.

'None of your business,' says Kirsty.

'What's it like?'

'None of your business.'

'Unless you get some qualifications, you'll always be in dead-end jobs.'

'Who says it's a dead end? I might be made manager soon.'

'Yes, but of what?'

'None of your business.'

'The thing is,' says Toby, patiently, 'it doesn't have to be A levels, or university or all that. Now's the chance, in the sixth form, to talk to the careers people, work out a proper plan or get some vocational training, something which will suit your talents.'

'Don't give me all that shit,' says Kirsty. 'I haven't got any talents. You're talking like that drip Witting.'

'Well then, we want you to come back,' says Toby, looking very solemn. 'All your friends. Yeah, I know I'm a new one, but honestly, they all miss you . . .'

Kirsty looks at his face, so serious, then she gets up and gives him a quick kiss. She opens the door to find her mother, just by chance, is standing behind it, pretending to sweep the floor.

'Mum, what are you doing?' says Kirsty.

'What are you doing?' says her mother, all worried, looking at both of them.

'None of your business,' says Kirsty to her mother. Then she turns to Toby. 'And that's your answer as well, Toby. But thanks for coming.'

She gives Toby another kiss, in front of her mother, who now looks confused rather than worried. Then Kirsty shows Toby to the door and lets him out.

Regents Park Fitness Club, same day, early afternoon

Mrs Scott-Scott has gone to the bank. Things are fairly quiet this afternoon. Kirsty is sitting thinking, about life and the future, time and space, rents and deposits, school and work. The front-door buzzer goes. 'I want to speak to Kirsty,' says a voice.

'Who is it?' asks Kirsty. It sounds to her like a boy, possibly Toby, and she certainly does not want to talk to him again, though she finds some of his remarks still queuing up in her head.

'Kirsty, is that you?' says the voice.

Kirsty gets up and goes to the office, to train the video on the front door and activate the secret overhead camera (very useful should the police call, so Mrs Scott-Scott has told Kirsty). The office is locked. Mrs Scott-Scott has taken the keys. Kirsty goes back to the buzzer phone.

'I say there, do hurry up.' The voice has now gone deeper, much posher.

'Who is it?' says Kirsty. 'What's your number?'

'Cucumber,' says the voice, then starts laughing.

'I must have a name, then,' says Kirsty.

'Okay then,' says the voice. 'It's your friend . . . Raae . . .' The last name has been whispered, confidentially, and not all that clearly.

'Colonel Ronny?' asks Kirsty. She presses the button to open the door. She has been told by Mrs Scott-Scott to be extra polite to the Colonel because of his contacts, even if he does arrive a bit too merry after some of his lunches.

The figure who comes in is not the Colonel, unless he is playing one of his silly tricks. He is wearing a very old and tattered raincoat, sunglasses, a trilby and a joke moustache.

It takes only a brief second for Kirsty to realize who it is.

'Look, bugger off,' she says. 'You'll get me the sack.'

'I'm a customer,' he says. 'I've got money, ha ha.'

'Pinched it, I should think,' says Kirsty.

'You can't chuck me out, I want to become a member.'

'You're not old enough,' says Kirsty.

'But I'm big enough,' he says, taking off his hat and his shades.

'Go on, get out.'

'No, I've a right to be here,' he says. 'Just as much as you.'

The figure begins to unbutton his raincoat. He is naked underneath, apart from boxer shorts and a package strapped to his chest.

'I've brought these for you,' he says. 'Madame.'

It is Raffy. He heavily stresses the word 'madame', just in case Kirsty has missed his joke. Then he unties the parcel, which has become rather squashed, and hands it to her. Kirsty opens the parcel and bursts out laughing. Inside are seventeen red roses, one for every year of her life. A bit premature, as her birthday is not until next week, 1 October, but how kind, how thoughtful of Raffy to remember. Or someone in her class to remember.

'With my apologies,' says Raffy, 'for all the horrible things I've said and done in the past. And probably will do and say again in the future, tra la, so it goes, but I mean it, honest . . .'

He gives Kirsty a kiss. The buzzer goes again.

'Quick, get your stupid coat on,' says Kirsty. 'This is a respectable establishment.'

The front door opens before Kirsty can press the button. It is Mrs Scott-Scott, letting herself in with her own key. Raffy pushes past her and gets out of the door.

'Who was that?' says Mrs Scott-Scott, when he has gone.

'New member,' says Kirsty, looking down at her book. 'Gave his name as Banks, of St Andrews Road. Don't believe it, personally. I think he was in some sort of disguise. He could be plain clothes police . . .'

'Hmm,' says Mrs Scott-Scott. 'We might close early tonight, as a precaution.'

'In that case could I have my money now?' asks Kirsty. 'I'd like to leave early anyway . . .'

School, sixth-form common room, Monday mid-morning

There are not many people around, except those

with a free period. Naturally, they are sitting quietly, working hard, as studious sixth formers should. The silence is quite eerie. Sam breaks it, returning to a conversation he started earlier. 'Actually, he's thinking of doing it on Sundays as well,' says Sam. 'His boring old clothes are going a bomb.'

'That's good,' says Kirsty.

'If he hires a stall for the two days, instead of just Saturday, he gets it a bit cheaper. So you could run it both days, if you want. Be double the money.'

'Great,' says Kirsty. 'I can save my earnings.' She goes back to the chapter in her Sociology textbook, 'Work as the Opiate of the Masses'. Sam returns to his English essay, 'How Romantic were the Romantics?'

The silence is finally broken again by the arrival of Raffy. He usually does manage to interrupt all silences, disturb most atmospheres, just by his presence. But this time he does have some news. 'I've seen the list, Kirsty,' he shouts across the room. 'You've passed probation. Great, eh? In fact everyone has. He's put it up early; very strange. I really think Banko has gone soft in the head in his old age, or soft in his bum.'

'Hey, that's good, Kirsty,' says Sam.

Kirsty smiles and returns to her book. Silence seeps back. The common room slumbers. Even Raffy sits down and settles himself, not to his books, but to thoughts of his Saturday-morning job. Tomorrow morning he plans to make a few calls, nose around the office. He is beginning to suspect that Taz's father not only owns the shop but perhaps a dodgy massage parlour as well.

Kirsty is concentrating, being a newly reformed student, putting all thoughts of the last three weeks out of her head. She has even shoved to the back of her mind that image of the surprise client in Natasha's cubicle. She has told no one about him. But the information has obviously come in handy to help her through probation, and who knows – it may prove useful again, one of these days, one of these terms, as Kirsty and her friends progress through the sixth form.

In the next exciting S.T.A.R.S. book, will Kirsty and Raffy become close friends again? What happens when Raffy forms a pop group? Why is he being so kind to Ella? And what on earth will Sam think? Not forgetting Jules, Dim, Colette, Toby. And the mysterious Taz . . .

THE END

Some other books you might enjoy

CAN'T STOP US NOW

Fran Lantz

Can four girls make it in the music business? Reg Barthwaite, pop promoter and manager, knows he's on a winner when he picks CC, Robin, Gail and Annette to form a new rock band. But soon they discover that making it in the music business isn't that easy, and as Reg becomes ever more insistent that they play on his terms, the girls are forced to question just what they want – fame at any price?

MAKING IT ON OUR OWN

Fran Lantz

It's not long since CC, Robin, Gail and Annette – Overnight Sensation – were the talk of the music press, but to them that seems like years ago.

Now they're on their own, no manager and no record company, just four girls, their music and lots of determination. Suddenly everything is happening for them. How can they cope with the trauma of leaving home? They've got to find jobs to pay for the band, carry on studying and find time for boyfriends! Can they fit all this in with their practice sessions and plans to cut a demo tape? And what about that elusive record contract?

A GIRL LIKE ABBY

Hadley Irwin

This isn't just another love story. Abby is trapped in her own nightmare world. Often she is 'absent' – not available – pulled far back inside herself in a world to which no one gains admittance. No one except Chip, who is let in just once and discovers her terrible secret . . . and he knows at once that he must do something to help her.

BUDDY

Nigel Hinton

Buddy would have given anything for a more conventional dad on the night of the meeting with his form teacher at school. In the past, his mum would go to these meetings on her own but she left home six months ago and hasn't been heard from since. It's a bewildering time for Buddy as he struggles to understand the adult world and come to terms with the embarrassment and the love that he feels for both his parents.

MEMORY

Margaret Mahy

Jonny sets out to find his dead sister's friend, after a night of trouble. But wandering through the streets late at night he finds Old Sophie West instead. Sophie suffers from senile dementia and is reduced to living on her own in genteel but dreadful squalor. As a temporary outcast himself, Jonny takes refuge with her. While Sophie has no memory at all, Jonny's memory of his sister's death is all too strong; their accidental meeting is about to change both their lives in a way they could never have imagined.

GOOD-NIGHT, PROF, LOVE

John Rowe Townsend

Graham is nearly seventeen, wears spectacles, and is destined for a boring life in his father's accountancy firm. Lynn works in Jeff's Cafe and never thinks more than a day ahead. Who would have thought their meeting over a cup of tea and a meat pie would lead to romance?

GIDEON AHOY!

William Mayne

Eva can't help remembering what Gideon was like when he was very young – before he was deaf, before he was ill. Now every morning she hears him give his strange, inarticulate morning shout and feels again the distance his brain damage has brought between them. And now Gideon is going to have a job – a real job in the outside world. How is he going to cope?

SECRETS AT SEVENTEEN

Jennifer Cole

It doesn't take Mollie and Cindy long to decide that Nicole is hiding something big. But when they think they know what the secret is, they get worried . . . What do you do if you think your sister is seeing an older man?

THIN ICE

Marc Talbert

Martin's biggest problem is Mr Raven. It's bad enough having a teacher interfere with his own private life, but when he finds out Mr Raven is secretly seeing *his mother*, it's more than Martin can handle.

FACING UP

Robin F. Brancato

Dave and Jep are the closest of friends. They are opposites in character but that makes life more interesting and Dave doesn't even mind Jep's girlfriend Susan tagging along. But things change when Susan makes a play for Dave. Torn between Jep's friendship and Susan's love, Dave feels sickened, but before he can explain to his friend a tragic accident changes everything, for ever.

DRUGS: WHY SAY NO?

Vanora Leigh

Drug abuse is affecting all types of people, from the rich and famous to the poor and unemployed, but especially the young. So a clear and informed understanding of the facts and issues involved is vital for all. This clear, straightforward and incisive book cuts through the maze of jargon, slang and conflicting opinion which surrounds the problem.

WHAT A WEEK – WITH BRUNO BROOKES

Mary Wilson

Bruno Brookes has his own weekday show and presents the live Sunday Chart Show to an audience of millions. But that's just the beginning! In this sort of life you need bundles of energy, but do you have any free time? Is it all as exciting as it looks?

ATTACKS OF OPINION

Terry Jones

Whether you agree or disagree with them, you can't ignore Terry Jones' *Attacks of Opinion*. Produced for the Young Guardian 'Input' column between 1987 and 1988, these satirical articles on topical and controversial issues are written in his own ironical, biting style, and are brilliantly complemented by Gerald Scarfe's satirical cartoons.

ON YOUR BIKE!

Merry Archard

Hankering after a holiday, a hi-fi, or drooling over the latest fashions? Well, get on your bike with these money-raising schemes and use your spare time and talents to boost your lifestyle.